TECHNICAL ANALYSIS TRADING

Making Money with charts

Published by: Network 18 PublicationPrivate Ltd, 507, Prabhat Kiran, 17, Rajendra Place, New Delhi -110008

Printed and Bound by: Print Plus Pvt. Ltd.

First Edition 2012

ISBN No. 978-93-80200-65-1

MRP Rs. 599/-

Disclaimer

While Network18 Publications and Network18 Group Companies the promoter of this Book, has taken due care and caution in compilation of information, generation of analysis and provision of expert recommendations appearing on this Book and/or provided to the subscribers of the Book by means such as sms/ Books/ print media or other electronic medium, we do not guarantee that such information is accurate, verified, adequate, current, complete or comprehensive. We disclaim all liability and responsibility for any inaccuracies, errors, omissions or representations appearing on this website or in the information delivered to subscribers by any means/media. Accordingly, your reliance and action based upon any of the information contained either in this Book or delivered to you by any means as part of this service is entirely at your own risk. The content appearing in the book or delivered to subscribers by any means is provided for information purposes only. The viewer/subscriber should independently verify the information before making any financial, trading or purchase decision or for any tax/ legal/ regulatory reporting. The statements appearing on our Book or delivered to you by any means, as part of this service, should not be regarded as an offer to sell or solicitation of an offer to purchase any products. This Book contains a number of links to other websites. In providing these links, Network18 Publications and Network18 Group Companies does not in any way endorse the contents of these other websites. Network18 Publications and Network18 Group Companies has not developedor reviewed the contents of those websites and does not accept any responsibility or liability for the contents of these other websites. Should you use a link from this website to any other website you do so entirely at your own risk. Network18 Publications and Network18 Group Companies does not endorse any advertisements appearing on this product Viewers/ subscribers/customers are advised that in relation to their use of the information either appearing on this Book or delivered to them by any means as part of this services, we will not be responsible or liable for delay in transmission of such information on account of failure of hardware, software or internet connectivity or other transmission problems. We will also not be responsible or liable in any way for delays, interruptions or failure in the delivery of sms or messages by print or electronic media to the subscriber's mobile phone/handset or postal address. The contents of this Book as well as information delivered to subscribers by any means as part of this service are Network18 Publications and Network18 Group Companies. You may not reproduce, redistribute, resell, broadcast or transfer all or any part of the contents of this website or information delivered to you by any means as part of this service, in any form or by any means whatsoever. We make no warranty that this Book or the messages delivered by electronic or mobile media as part of this services is free from viruses or anything else which has destructive properties and you will be solely responsible for any damage to your computer system or loss of data that results from your use of this service. Network18 Publications and Network18 Group Companies hereby also expressly disclaims any implied warranties under laws of any jurisdiction, to the extent permitted. Network18 Publications and Network18 Group Companies reserves the right to modify its Book (including this disclaimer) and the terms and conditions of use of the services provided by this Network18 Publications and Network18 Group Companies at any time without any liability. By viewing, subscribing to or using this service you are deemed to hereby accept this disclaimer. Network18 Publications and Network18 Group Companies reserves the right to take legal action, as deemed fit, if the terms and conditions of the use of this Book or its services as described herein are not compiled with. Any disputes in relation thereof shall be subject to the exclusive jurisdiction of the courts at Mumbai, India. Network18 Publications and Network18 Group Companies and content providers have no financial liability whatsoever to the users of this Book. For more information contact Network18 Publications and Network18 Group Companies at cd@network18online.com

CONTENTS

Disclaimer

Foreword

Technical analysis is all about interpreting charts towards arriving at insights on the probable future trends of prices. However, most reading material on technical analysis so far focuses less on charts and more on their interpretation. This book hopes to address that lacuna with a clear focus on what technical analysis is all about - CHARTS.

Lack of chart reading skills dents our real-time trading performance as opportunities could come and fade away even before we could spot a set-up. This book attempts to improve chart reading skills with over 150 chart based case studies. These charts are handpicked from across geographies, asset classes and timeframes.

Technical analysis is also about identifying patterns that have produced consistent results over a period of time. That's why this book delineates top patterns, puts them in the form of charts and supports them with detailed explanations, performance reports and case studies. In fact, the objective of this book is to help readers understand and trade during these typical set-ups, real-time!

Trading is simple and this book is an attempt to make it simpler.

Happy Reading!

CONTENTS

TECHNICAL ANALYSIS -
Basics

CHAPTER 1

Technical Analysis –
A Study of Demand and Supply

*T*echnical Analysis is the process of analysing the historical prices of an asset class in an effort to determine probable future prices. In other words, technical analysis is a study of demand and supply using charts. If there are more buyers than sellers, the demand for an asset class is greater than the supply and the price goes up. Conversely, if there are more sellers than buyers, the supply of the asset class is greater than the demand and the price goes down. This contest between buyers and sellers is recorded when we plot a chart which contains information on the movements of prices and volumes. Once we have these charts in front of us, with the knowledge of technical analysis, we can gain insights about the probable future trend of prices.

In short, Technical Analysis is a study of liquidity using charts.

Technical Analysis -
Assumptions

In order to understand technical analysis better, it's important to know the assumptions on which technical analysis is built -

Assumption 1

Everything is discounted and reflected in market prices

According to technical analysis, all fundamental, economic, political, psychological and other information is reflected in the price of an asset class.

Assumption 2

Prices tend to move in trends

Market prices move in one direction, up or down, creating a trend. That trend persists until the price movement reverses and starts moving in the opposite direction.

A technician, i.e. someone who practically uses technical analysis, believes that it is possible to identify a trend, invest based on the trend and then make money as the trend unfolds. And because technical analysis can be applied to many different time frames, it is possible to spot both short-term and long-term trends.

Assumption 3

Market action is repetitive

Basic human nature does not change and hence it tends to react to similar situations in a consistent way.

Technical Analysis - **Applications**

Technical analysis can be used to analyse price movements in all asset classes, i.e. stocks, bonds, options, futures, commodities and many other forms of investment. This analysis can be used to identify buy and sell opportunities. Technical analysis can also be a useful tool for a wide range of time horizons – from very short term to very long term perspectives.

TYPES OF TRADERS

There are three types of traders, differentiated on the basis of the timeframe they choose while trading: -

Swing Traders hold on to their trades from a few days to a couple of weeks, Position Traders hold their trades from a few weeks to months and, at times, even years and Day Traders square up their positions intraday; they don't even take overnight risks.

....

[1]*The term asset class means stocks, futures, options, commodities, bonds, foreign exchange or any other form of investment which is traded on an exchange*

....

TYPES OF CHARTS

Technical analysis records the contest between buyers and sellers in a chart form. Analysts examine these charts to track the historical prices of a particular stock in an effort to speculate on the future trends in prices. This is usually done by using one of the following types of charts –

- ➤ Bar charts
- ➤ Candle stick charts
- ➤ Line charts

One very important aspect of all technical analysis charts is that the Price scale is assigned to the vertical axis, while the horizontal axis carries the Time scale, which could be hourly, daily, weekly, etc.

BAR CHARTS

Bar charts convert price movements into easily readable charts. Usually four elements make up a bar chart (Fig 1.1)–

- ➤ Open (Opening Price)
- ➤ High (Highest Price)
- ➤ Low (Lowest Price)
- ➤ Close (Closing Price)

Elements of a bar chart

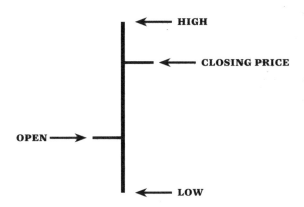

Fig 1.1

A price bar can represent any time frame, as per the user's requirements, from one minute to one month. Total vertical length/height of the bar represents the entire trading range for a particular period. The top of the bar represents the highest price of the period, while the lowest price during the period is depicted by the bottom of the bar. A small protrusion to the left of the bar represents the Open. Similarly, the Close for the session is shown by a small protrusion on the right side of the bar.

A standard bar chart looks like the Fig 1.2 that follows

A standard bar chart

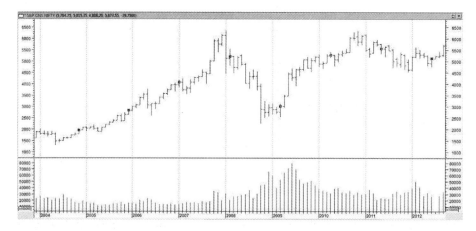

Fig 1.2

Chart 1.2 depicts the price data of Nifty from 2004 to 2012 in the form of a bar chart.

CANDLE STICK CHARTS

Candlestick charting has been used by Japanese traders for centuries. However, it is only recently that this technique has caught the attention of technicians worldwide. The Japanese Candlestick Line (Fig 1.3) uses the same data (open, high, low and close) to depict the price movements of a stock, but in a more visually appealing and comprehendible form. The thick part of a candlestick line is called the Real Body. It represents the range between the session's opening and closing prices. If the Real Body is red or black, it means that the close of the period was lower than the open. If the Real Body is green

TECHNICAL ANALYSIS

or white, it implies that the close was higher than the open. The lines above and below the body are called the Shadows. The Shadows represent the price extremes during the period. The Shadow above the Real Body is called the Upper Shadow, while the one below the Real Body is known as the Lower Shadow. The top of the Upper Shadow is the high of the day, whereas the bottom of the Lower Shadow is the day's low.

Elements of a candlestick chart

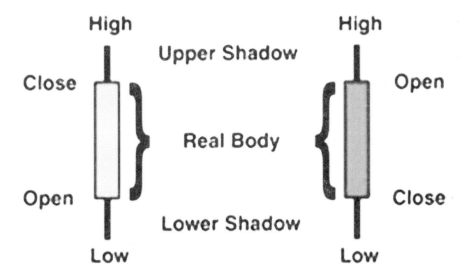

Fig 1.3

Candlesticks are visually appealing, and convey price information in a quicker, more efficient and easily comprehensible manner. It is upto the trader's individual discretion to use either candle charts or bar charts. Chart 1.4 below depicts the price data of NIFTY (monthly timeframe) in a candlestick chart form.

DJIA price movement on arithmetic scale

Nifty data in candlestick form

Fig 1.4

LINE CHARTS

Fig 1.6

Line charts only reflect the closing values on the timeframe we choose in a price chart.

Nifty data in line form

The above chart, Fig 1.6, shows the price movement of the DJIA from 1920 to 2010 on an arithmetic scale (quarterly intervals). On the other hand, Fig 1.7 shows the price movement on a log scale during the same period and with the same intervals i.e. quarterly. When we compare both the charts it is clear that the log scale gives more importance to percentage changes. For instance, the market crashed by 90 per cent in the late 1920s; this comes out very clearly from the log charts while a crash of such magnitude doesn't find a place on the arithmetic scale. Further, the correction that occurred in 2008 is prominent on the arithmetic scale as the number of points lost (approximately 7000 points) by the DJIA was more than the absolute number of points lost by the DJIA during the crash in the

Fig 1.5

Whether you use bar charts or candlestick charts, the period to be examined will depend upon your investment time frame - short, intermediate or long term. Though there is no generally accepted definition for these three terms, short term roughly refers to the next 3 months, the intermediate term stretches between 3 to 12 months and beyond 12 months is considered long term . Analysts use hourly and daily charts to determine price trends over the short term. Weekly charts are used to studying prices over the inter-mediate term, while prices over the long term are studied using monthly, quarterly and yearly charts.

it closed was higher than the open. The lines above and below the body are called the Shadows. The Shadows represent the price extremes during the period. The Shadow above the Real Body is called the Upper Shadow while the one below the Real Body is known as the Lower Shadow. The top of the Upper Shadow is the high of the day, whereas the bottom of the Lower Shadow is the day's low.

Elements of a candlestick chart

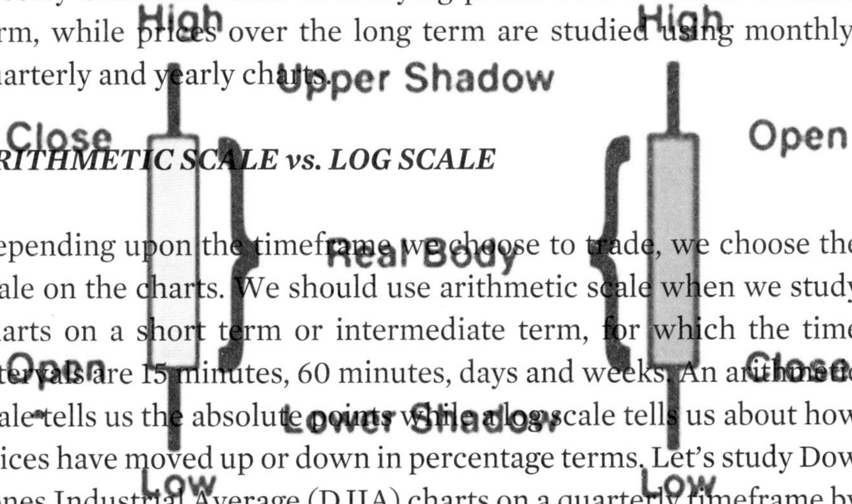

High · High · Close · Open · Upper Shadow · Real Body · Open · Close · Lower Shadow · Low · Low

ARITHMETIC SCALE vs. LOG SCALE

Depending upon the timeframe we choose to trade, we choose the scale on the charts. We should use arithmetic scale when we study charts on a short term or intermediate term, for which the time intervals are 15 minutes, 60 minutes, days and weeks. An arithmetic scale tells us the absolute points while a log scale tells us about how prices have moved up or down in percentage terms. Let's study Dow Jones Industrial Average (DJIA) charts on a quarterly timeframe by using both the arithmetic scale and the log scale.

Fig 1.3

Candlesticks are visually appealing, and convey price information in a quicker, more efficient and easily comprehensible manner. It is upto the trader's individual discretion to use either candle charts or bar charts. Chart 1.4 below depicts the price data of NIFTY (monthly timeframe) in a candlestick chart form.

DJIA price movement on arithmetic scale

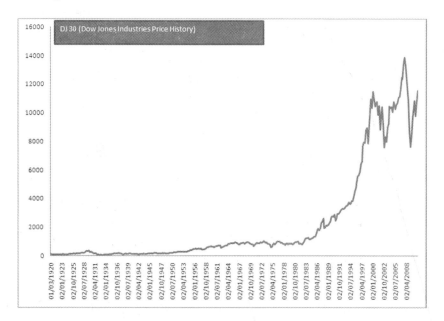

Fig 1.6

The above chart, Fig 1.6, shows the price movement of the DJIA from 1920 to 2010 on an arithmetic scale (quarterly intervals). On the other hand, Fig 1.7 shows the price movement on a log scale during the same period and with the same intervals i.e. quarterly. When we compare both the charts it is clear that the log scale gives more importance to percentage changes. For instance, the market crashed by 90 per cent in the late 1920s; this comes out very clearly from the log charts while a crash of such magnitude doesn't find a place on the arithmetic scale. Further, the correction that occurred in 2008 is prominent on the arithmetic scale as the number of points lost (approximately 7000 points) by the DJIA was more than the absolute number of points lost by the DJIA during the crash in the late 1920s (around 450 points).

In short, it's better to apply a log scale when we study price movements over the long term, i.e. when we use monthly, quarterly or yearly charts, while it is preferable to use the arithmetic scale when we study charts over the short to intermediate term.

DJIA price movement on log scale

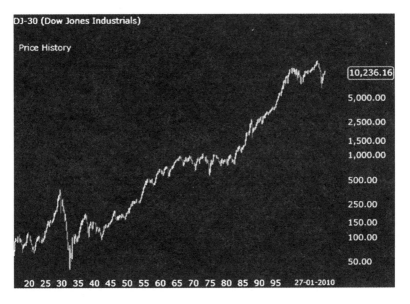

Fig 1.7

TYPES OF TRENDS

Technical analysis is based on the fact that the prices of stocks move in fairly definite trends. This phenomenon is true for price trends of individual stocks and the market as a whole. These trends can be up, down or sideways (Fig 1.8).

The primary tools that are used to identify trends are:

→ Trend lines
→ Pivots

TRENDLINE

Trend lines are an important tool in technical analysis for both trend identification and confirmation. Technicians use trend lines in two ways: first, to identify the direction of the movement of stock prices; second, to determine if and when the movement will change.

A trend line is a straight line that connects two or more price points and then extends into the future to act as a line of support or a resistance level, as explained later. In fact, technicians look to trend lines for their ability to support price declines or resist price advances.

Trendlines

 Image 1

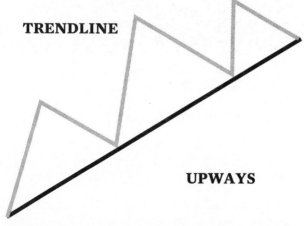

Image 2

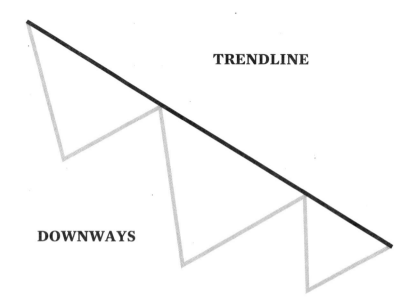

TRENDLINE

DOWNWAYS

Image 3

TRENDLINE

Fig 1.8

SIDEWAYS

Trendlines can be categorized as follows:

A Downtrendline(Fig 1.8, Image 2) is a line that connects two or more highs in a price chart. A Downtrend is characterized by a sequential decrease in maximum prices. It can also be considered as a descending resistance level: Bears set the pace as they push prices down. A break above the downtrend line indicates that net-supply is decreasing and that a change of trend could be imminent. Fig 1.9 is a DJIA candlesticks chart which shows how a downtrend line is drawn.

DJIA candlesticks chart with a downtrendline

Fig 1.9

An **uptrendline** (Fig 1.8, Image 1) is a line that connects two or more lows in a price chart. An Uptrend is characterized by a sequential increase in minimum prices. It can also be considered as ascending support level: Bulls set the pace as they push prices up. A break below the uptrend line indicates that net-demand has weakened and a change in the trend could be imminent. Chart 1.10 is a DJIA line chart and shows how an uptrend line is plotted.

DJIA line chart with an uptrendline

Fig 1.10

A **sideways pattern** (Fig 1.8, Image 3) represents stability between supply and demand in the marketplace. Trendlines in this type of market, often referred to as a narrow trading range or congestive phase, are drawn by connecting both the highs and lows. Prices in this type of market can break upward or downward so it is valuable to establish the top and bottom of the range as it could set the stage for a sharp move once the sideways trend is broken. This is signaled by a price break through a well-established trend line. Fig 1.11 illustrates a sideways pattern, when prices moved in a narrow range between 1975 and 1985 on DJIA charts, and a sharp upmove that followed once the range was broken.

DJIA chart with sideways trend lines

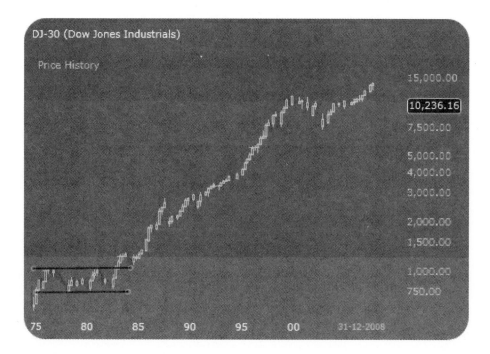

Fig 1.11

A trend is assumed to be in effect until it gives definite signals that it has reversed. No trend continues forever. Technical analysts are as concerned with the breaking of trendlines as they are with watching a trend continue.

PIVOTS - TRADING THE DOW THEORY

The foundation of pivots was laid by Charles Dow in the early 1900s when he defined trends.

Using pivots we study trends as follows:

An uptrend (Fig 1.13, Image 1) on a chart of any timeframe is characterized by a series of higher highs (higher tops) and higher lows (higher bottoms) in prices OR by a break in a lower high formation in a downtrend. A Downtrend (Fig 1.13, Image 2) occurs on successive lower highs (lower tops) and lower lows (lower bottoms) OR By a break in a higher low formation in a uptrend.

A sideways trend (Fig 1.13, Image 3) has relatively equal highs and lows, i.e. it represents a range-bound market.

It has been found that pivots perform much better than trendlines as predictors of future price trends, even on a standalone basis.

Trendlines

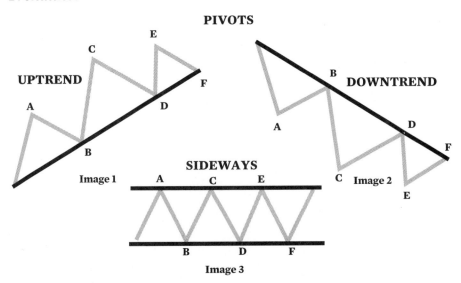

Fig 1.12

All the points i.e. higher high, higher low, lower high and lower low are called pivots (in the above image points a,b,c,d,e and f are pivots).

PIVOTS ILLUSTRATED

Chart 1.14 is a EUR/USD spot chart with a weekly timeframe and all the points, i.e. higher highs (HT or higher top), higher lows (HB or higher bottom), lower highs (LT or lower top), lower lows (LB or lower bottom) on the chart are pivots.

Euro/USD spot chart (weekly timeframe)

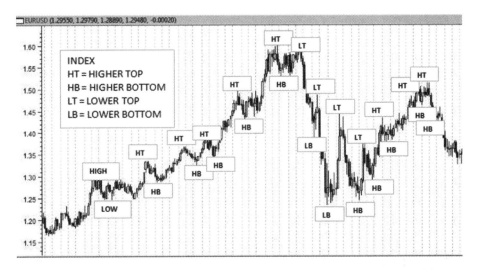

Fig 1.13

SUPPORT AND RESISTANCE

Support represents demand zones and resistance represents supply zones. At support levels, we find a level of demand for a stock or currency or commodity that stops the prices from falling further. Similarly, at resistance levels we find a level of supply that stops prices from rising further. Support levels are reaction lows and resistance levels are reaction highs.

In an uptrend, support levels hold (or keep rising) while resistance levels are repeatedly broken and in a downtrend resistance levels hold (or keep falling) while support levels are repeatedly broken. A break in a support level in an uptrend or a break in a resistance level in a downtrend triggers a change in the trend.

CASE STUDY:

Fig 1.14 is a Nifty futures chart with daily intervals. According to trendline analysis, the lines cd and gh are supports while the resistance lines are ab, ef and ij. As on Oct 09, the support line for Nifty futures is line gh and according to trendline analysis, a break below this line ends the uptrend.

Nifty futures chart with daily intervals

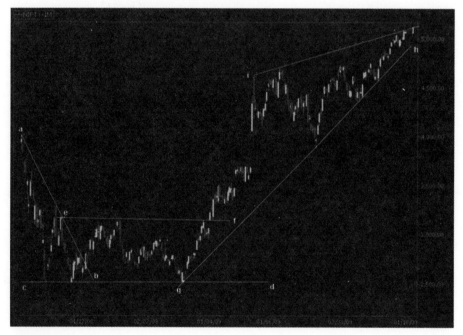

Fig 1.14

CASE STUDY

According to pivot analysis, all the lows (be it higher lows or lower

TECHNICAL ANALYSIS

lows) are support zones and all the highs (be it higher highs or lower highs) are resistance zones. As we can see from the Nifty weekly chart (Fig 1.15), the Nifty got into a downtrend after breaking a higher low (support) of around 5500 on January 2008 and later entered an uptrend around 2970-3000 only after it broke a lower high (resistance) on March 2009. According to pivots, the uptrend that started around 3000 was broken when the higher low, at around 5900, was taken out in November 2010.

Nifty weekly chart

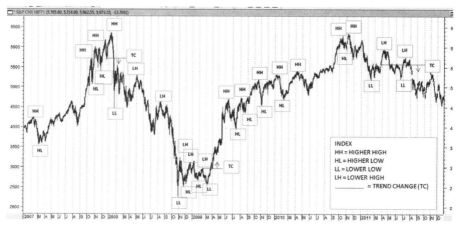

Fig. 1.15

Exercises

Technical Analysis Basics

1) **What are the Key Technical Analysis Assumptions?**

A) Everything is discounted and reflected in market prices

B) Prices don't trend.

C) Market action is repetitive

D) Price tends to move in trends.

Answer Options: 1) A, C & D **2)** A,B,C & D **3)** A,B & C

Answer: ☐1

---

2) **What scale do we use to study price movements over long-term?**

A) Everything is discounted and reflected in market prices

A) Price Scale

B) Log Scale

C) Arithmetic Scale

Answer: ☐B

---

3) **Can you draw an uptrend line which starts near 01/08/2009 and ends near 01/04/2011?**

A) No uptrend spotted

B)   We can draw a downtrend line between the subject periods

C)   Uptrend line can be drawn

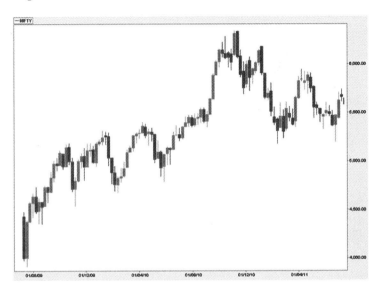

Answer: | **c) Uptrend line can be drawn as shown below** |

ADVANCED TECHNICAL ANALYSIS

CHAPTER 2

Key patterns in a price chart

*T*here are six key formations or set-ups that trigger a trend change (from up to down or down to up), in any asset class (i.e. stocks, bonds, currency, commodities, index futures, options, etc), across timeframes and intervals(1 minute, 5 minute, weekly, quarterly and so on). These set-ups can be spotted, in all up moves or down moves, in the price charts of any asset class globally. They are:-

• PIVOTS

• GAPS

• HEAD AND SHOULDERS

• DOUBLE TOP AND DOUBLE BOTTOM

• IRREGULAR DIAGONALS

• SPIKES

Knowledge of the Dow Theory and the ability to draw trendlines is integral to understanding these six set-ups. Spikes, unlike the other set-ups listed above, cannot be traded.

HOW THESE KEY PATTERNS WERE IDENTIFIED

Technical analysis is based on the principle that market action is repetitive due to the human tendency to react to similar situations in a consistent way.

This is the reason why fairly identifiable and repetitive chart patterns frequently develop, thereby helping us understand a continuation of the existing trend or alerting us to an imminent change in the trend.

First let's understand what benchmarks are used to identify a pattern as a key pattern.

A set-up is classified as a key set-up if it satisfies five criteria, namely, significance, frequency, absolute points made, relevance and percentage wins.

- **Significance:** Is the set-up seen in all major tops and bottoms across asset classes? If it is, it can be considered a key pattern.

- **Frequency:** Does the set-up appear frequently on the charts across timeframes? A key pattern will appear irrespective of the timeframe.

- **Absolute points made:** How many points has the pattern

made in the past across timeframes? The greater the number of points made, the more certain that the set-up is a key pattern.

- **Relevance:** Does the performance of the set-up vary between asset classes, between constituents of the asset class and between market geographies? To be a key pattern, the set-up should have the same level of performance irrespective of where it is applied.

- **Percentage wins:** What is the win to loss ratio of the pattern in the period of testing its past performance (back-test)? A key pattern must have a high win:loss ratio.

In short, the test of a key pattern is its consistency of performance.

Popularly used patterns have been demonstrated in this book and supplemented with detailed explanations, case studies and charts.

Most importantly, this book will have achieved its purpose once you are able to use your own discretion and form your own personal judgement about which patterns should be included as part of your trading system. This ability to discern will come to you once you have understood the tenets of technical analysis and tried and tested them out on your own with the help of the exercises provided herein.

ABOUT TRADING SYSTEMS

–What is a trading system? A trading system is a system designed with a precise entry, an exit, position sizing and stop–loss levels. Trading systems are built after back-testing various parameters and these parameters might include absolute and percentage gains delivered by the system during the subject period, time taken by the system to achieve its target, timeframe that has delivered the maximum points, choice of filters, position size to be used, etc.

The timeframe chosen to back-test a trading system always depends upon the investment horizon. A day trader might choose intra-day timeframes like 5 minutes, 10 minutes or an hour to back test, while an investor might choose weekly or monthly timeframes to back test.

Trading systems can be either manual or automated. A manual system involves a trader sitting at the computer screen, looking for signals and interpreting whether to buy or sell. In an automated trading system, the trader "teaches" the software what signals to look for and how to interpret them. It is thought that automated trading takes the detrimental human element of psychology out of trading.

Developing a trading system is an important activity and a pre-requisite to start investing or trading any asset class. In short, not having a trading system is like crossing a highway with your eyes closed.

BUILDING A TRADING SYSTEM

A trading system is always built based around an idea. This idea may or may not be related to technical analysis at all but it's extremely important to back-test the idea and test how well it would have performed if it were implemented in the past. The practice of back-testing, building a system around the back-test results and trading such systems in live markets is called Evidence Based Trading.

It's also important to understand that in the process of building a trading system we might also lose a substantial part of our trading capital. So, it's important to play it safe till we find the right idea, back-test the idea thoroughly and build a trading system around it. This book has a lot of set-ups that have a good track record of consistent performance across asset classes and the idea could just be to back-test the top set-ups discussed in this book on any of your favourite asset classes. This could help you build a trading system around it. As you go along, you will find that some set-ups, like pivots (refer pages 54 to 57 of this book), can give great results in one asset-class and poor results in another. Our core objective is to trade set-ups in the asset classes and timeframes in which they work best.

IMPORTANCE OF TESTING PAST PERFORMANCE

That leaves us with a critical question: How do I test the past performance (back-test) of my idea? If you are more comfortable with a manual back-test, then just check for the set-ups visually on the asset class you trade. Also back-test as many timeframes as possible and once you find that the idea works best on a particular timeframe then stick to that timeframe only. Back-testing should be done for at least 2 years, if you are an intra-day trader. If you are an intermediate or a long term trader, then you must back-test for at least 10 years before you apply your idea in the live markets. You must back-test for the frequency points made, time taken to hit your target, number of times the stop-loss limit has been hit and so on. How to go about a back-test will be dealt with in different sections of this book. Back-test sheets have been included in some sections to help you appreciate the importance of evidence based trading and back-testing.

Now, another crucial question: What is the guarantee that the idea we have back-tested (the one that has performed well in the past) will repeat its success or perform in the future? Let's recollect what we read on page 1 of this book "market actions are repetitive". This simply means that basic human nature does not change and hence, it tends to react to similar situations in consistent ways. For example, whenever there is a stock market crash, the price of gold invariably shoots up as investors' aversion to risk takes centre stage. Since the market price is a reflection of human greed and fear, analysts study it to determine how people react under certain conditions. These emotions, in turn, get reflected in the movement of prices and thus, enable anticipation of future price movements. Nature in itself is repetitive – We have waves on the beach *always*, the sun rises in the east and sets in the west *always*, we have gravity on our planet always and we have oxygen to breathe *always*..... In fact, if nature stops being repetitive, we would all stop functioning!

PIVOTS – USING THE DOW THEORY TO TRADE

●

CHAPTER 3

Pivots –
Trading The Dow Theory

" *I* never try to predict or anticipate. I only try to react to what the market is telling me by its behavior"-

Jesse Livermore(Known as the Great bear of Wall Street, Jesse made several multi-million dollar fortunes during market crashes in 1907 and 1929)

When we use Technical Analysis, we are not concerned with where the money comes from but we are certainly interested in what the money is doing! We want to know whether its pushing the markets up or down... Pivots help to figure this out and enable us to trade in the direction of the money flow...**in short, Pivots represent the ultimate source of demand and supply in a price chart.**

PIVOTS EXPLAINED:

Hold your right hand in front of your face with your palm towards you. You will see that your ring finger makes a higher top and bottom than your little finger. Then you can see that your middle finger has higher top and bottom than your ring finger. Taken together, those three fingers represent a **RALLY.**

Now, your index finger makes a lower top and lower bottom than your middle finger and your thumb makes a lower top and bottom than your index finger. Here you have a DECLINE. The highest point of your middle finger together with the two lower tops on both sides (the top of your ring finger and index finger) form a **PIVOT.**

Now here's another type of Pivot. Flip your palm around so that your fingers are pointing towards the ground and your palm is still towards your face. The lowest point of the middle finger and the two higher bottoms on both sides (your ring finger and index finger) also form a **PIVOT.**

Pivots

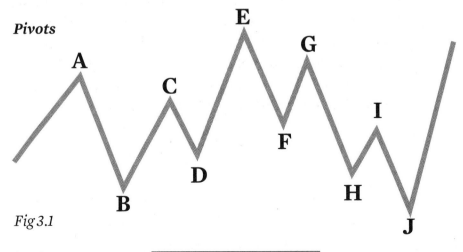

Fig 3.1

In the above image, points A ,B ,C, D ,E, F,G, H, I and J are pivots. **The dictionary defines pivots as the "central point around which something turns".**

The same is applicable even to TA but the key to identifying pivots is that they should be visually obvious turn around points in a price chart of any timeframe.

US/JPY monthly chart

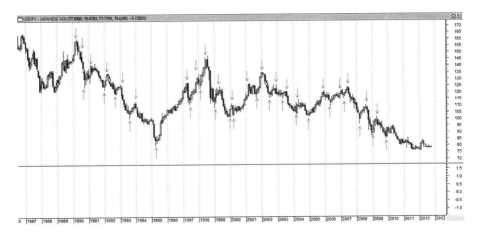

Fig 3.2

In the above, USD/JPY monthly chart all the points represented by the arrow marks are pivots. As you can see, all these points are visually obvious turnaround points.

Euro/USD weekly chart

INDEX
HT = HIGHER TOP
HB = HIGHER BOTTOM
LT = LOWER TOP
LB = LOWER BOTTOM

Fig 3.3

In the above chart, all the points represented by high, low, HT, HB, LT and LB are pivots; these are points at which the price trend turns around, i.e. prices that were moving up start going down after touching such points and prices that were moving down start going up after touching such points.

Using pivots we study trends as follows:

An Uptrend on a price chart of any timeframe is characterized by a series of higher highs (higher tops) and higher lows (higher bottoms).

TECHNICAL ANALYSIS

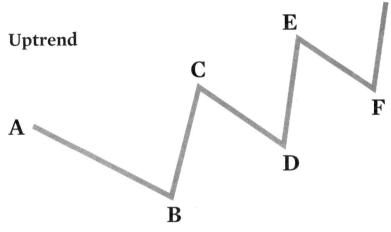

Uptrend

Fig 3.4

In an uptrend, we have HIGHER PIVOT LOWS(or higher pivot bottoms)

In figure 3.4, you will see that the highs – A, C and E – are consecutively higher. At the same time, the lows – B, D and F - are consecutively lower.

We, therefore, have an uptrend.

To reiterate, the points i.e. higher tops (point A , point C and point E) and higher bottoms (point B , point D and point F) are called pivots and together, they form an uptrend.

A **Downtrend** occurs when there are successive lower highs (lower tops) and lower lows (lower bottoms) in prices of any asset class of any timeframe.

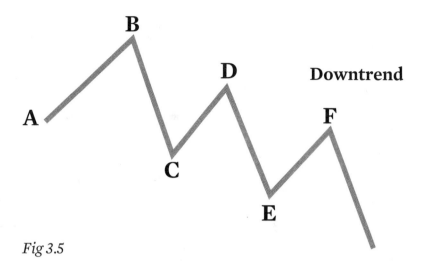

Fig 3.5

In figure 3.5, you will see that the lows – A, C and E – are consecutively lower. At the same time, the highs – B, D and F - are consecutively lower too.

The first decline starts from point B and ends with point C. Then a rally follows to a point that is lower than point B. We call this new point where the stock has rallied to as point D. And this trend continues into a downtrend. In a downtrend, we have lower pivot highs(or lower pivot tops)

As in the case of the uptrend, all the points i.e. lower tops (point B , point D and point F) and lower bottoms (point A , point C and point E) are called pivots and together they form a downtrend.

A **Sideways** trend has relatively equal highs and lows and represents a rangebound market.

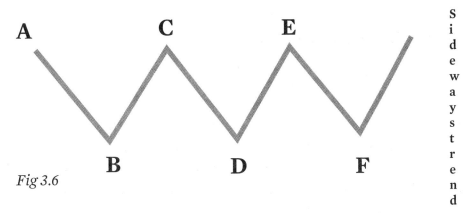

Fig 3.6

All the points in the above image points A,B,C,D,E and F are pivots and together they form a sideways trend.

How an uptrend gets triggered on the charts

An uptrend (as shown in Fig 3.7) gets triggered by a break in a lower high (lower top) formation in a downtrend

Uptrend triggered

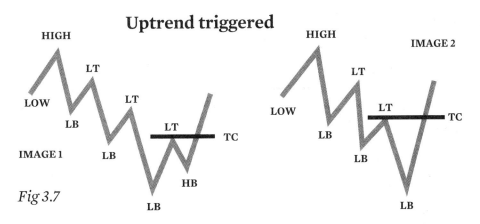

Fig 3.7

INDEX (above images)

LB = LOWER BOTTOM,LT = LOWER TOP,HB = HIGHER

BOTTOM,TC = TREND CHANGE

General rule for trading in an uptrend

If you trade by entering at a trend change, you could set a stop loss at the nearest pivotal bottom. In Image 1 of Fig 3.7, the stop loss can be set at HB area and as per Image 2, the stop loss can be set at the most recent LB prior to trend change. The buy that gets generated at a trend change will be covered only when a downtrend gets triggered

How a downtrend gets triggered on the charts

A downtrend (as shown in the below images) gets triggered by a break in a higher bottom (higher low) formation in an uptrend.

Downtrend triggered

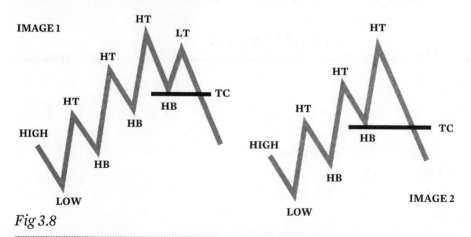

Fig 3.8

---

[1]A stop loss is an order placed with a broker to sell a security when it reaches a certain price. This mechanism is designed to limit an investor's loss on a security position. It is also known as a "stop order" or "stop-market order".

TECHNICAL ANALYSIS

INDEX (above image)

HT = HIGHER TOP, LT = LOWER TOP, HB = HIGHER BOTTOM, TC = TREND CHANGE

General rule for trading in a downtrend

The stop loss for the trade entered into at a trend change should be the nearest pivotal top. In Image 1, the stop loss can be set at LT and as per Image 2 the stop loss can be set at the most recent HT prior to trend change. The sell that gets generated at a trend change will be covered only when an uptrend gets triggered.

HOW TO TRADE THE TREND USING PIVOTS

Nifty weekly chart

Fig 3.9

In the above chart, which is a Nifty weekly chart, the downtrend got triggered by a break in the higher low formation (indicated by the TC with a down-arrow in the above charts) in Jan 08, while the Nifty was at around 5500 levels. Hence you can sell at this level and cover this sell only when an uptrend gets triggered.

The uptrend in the chart was triggered when the Nifty was at around 3000 –levels (as indicated by TC with an up arrow in the above charts). This uptrend was triggered due to a break in the lower high formation. Once an uptrend gets triggered, we must hold the buy trade and keep raising the stops to the nearest higher low.

Financial Technologies price chart (weekly)

Fig 3.10

Chart: Financial Technology

Entry point: The entry level was around 2200 and the down arrow in the above chart marks the entry into a sell trade. The impetus for the entry was the break in the Higher Bottom (HB), which is a sign of increasing supply.

Stop loss levels at entry: The nearest pivotal high (in this case a Lower Top marked as LT in the chart) prior to the sell trade should be chosen as the stop-loss level. In the chart, the stop-loss will be around 2700.

Exit Point: The exit level for the trade, which was entered into at 2200 will be around 550. In the above chart, the exit level is marked by an up arrow. Please note that since we entered with a sell trade here, we have to execute a buy trade to exit.

GMR Infra price chart (weekly)

Fig 3.11

Entry point: The entry level was around 110 and the down arrow in the above chart marks the entry into the sell trade. The impetus for the entry was a break in the Higher Low (HL), which is a sign of increasing supply.

Stop loss levels at entry: The nearest pivotal high (in this case a Lower High marked as LH) prior to the sell trade should be the stop-loss level. In the chart the stop-loss will be around 130.

Exit Point: The exit level for the trade, which was entered into at 110, will be around 40. In the above chart, the exit level is marked by an up arrow. Here, since we are covering our sell trade, a buy trade is placed.

SBI price chart (weekly)

Fig 3.12

Entry point: The entry level was around 1200 and the up arrow in the above chart marks the entry into a buy trade. You will notice that the SBI chart was making consistent lower highs (LH) till this point and the entry was triggered by a break in the Higher Low (HL) which is a sign of increasing demand.

Stop loss levels at entry: The nearest pivotal low (in this case a

TECHNICAL ANALYSIS

lower low marked as LL) prior to the buy trade will be the stop-loss level. In the chart, the stop-loss will be around 900.

Exit Point: The exit level for the trade, entered into at 1200 will be around 3000. In the above chart, the exit level is marked by a down arrow. Please note that since we are covering our buy trade here, a sell trade is placed.

DJIA chart (quarterly)

Fig 3.13

Entry point: The entry level was around 1000 and the up arrow in the above chart marks the entry into a buy trade. You will see from the above Dow Jones chart that the market was going through a long period of consolidation between 1966 and 1982 before the buy trade was signaled.

Stop loss levels at entry: The nearest pivotal low (in this case a higher low marked as HL) prior to the buy trade will be the stop-loss level. In the chart the stop-loss will be around 800.

Exit point: The exit level for the trade entered into at 1000 will be around 7000. In the above chart, the exit level is marked by a down arrow. Since we are covering our buy trade here, a sell trade is placed.

Note: As highlighted in chapter 1 we only use log charts to study charts with relatively long timeframes; therefore, as the above chart has a quarterly time frame, we use a log chart.

Euro/USD chart (weekly)

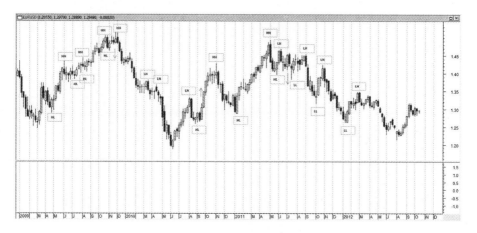

Fig 3.14

Entry points: The first entry was a sell trade and it came in at around 1.45 levels in Nov 2009. This is denoted by the first down arrow in the above chart. The second entry was a cover buy trade (Since we have already entered with a sell trade in Nov 2009, we would have to buy twice the quantity of the initial sell trade. This would enable us to unwind our initial sell position and enter a fresh buy position) and came at around 1.33 levels in Sep 2010. This is denoted by an up arrow in the above chart. The third entry was a cover sell trade and came at around 1.40 levels in July 2011. This is denoted by the second down arrow in the above chart.

Stop loss levels at entry: The nearest pivotal high in the case of a sell trade and the nearest pivotal low in the case of a buy trade will be suitable stop loss levels.

Exit Point: The exit level for each trade in the above chart eventually becomes the entry point for the next trade.This type of trading is called Stop And Reverse (SAR) as we keep following the price direction and go with the flow. While we exit specific trades, we never actually exit the market. We usually place SAR trades (the exit for one trade becomes the entry to the next trade) when we are following pivot based trading.

RCom price chart (weekly)

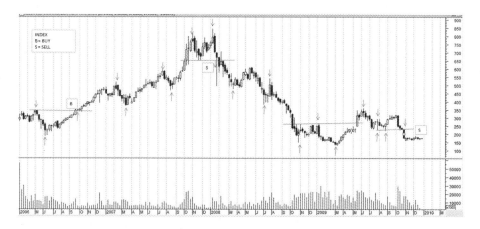

Fig 3.15

Entry points: The first entry was a buy trade and came in around 350 levels in Sep 2006. This is denoted by a Buy (B followed by up arrow in the above chart). Remember that we must keep raising our stops in case of a buy trade to the nearest higher low in case of a buy trade (all up arrows in the above chart are pivotal lows). The second entry was a cover sell trade (as mentioned in the previous case study, we have to sell twice the quantity of the initial buy trade as we have to unwind our buy position and place a fresh sell trade) and came at around 650 levels in Jan 2008. This is denoted by a down arrow (S followed by a down arrow in the above chart). Remember that we keep lowering our stops to the nearest pivotal high in case of a sell trade (all down arrows in the above chart are pivotal highs). The third entry was a cover sell trade and came at around 250 levels in Oct 2009. This is denoted by the last down arrow (followed by S) in the above chart.

Stop loss levels at entry: The nearest pivotal high in case of a sell trade and nearest pivotal low in case of a buy trade are suitable stop loss levels.

Exit Point: As mentioned in the previous case study, we placed SAR trades (the exit for one trade becomes the entry into the next trade) here as well.

Gold chart (Daily)

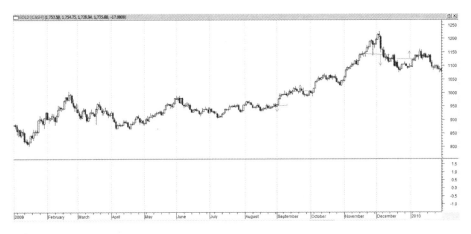

Fig 3.16

Entry points: The first entry was a buy trade and came in around 14,600 levels in July 2009. This is denoted by the first up arrow in the above chart. As we learnt in past cases, you would have to keep raising your stops to the nearest pivotal low as this was a buy trade. The second entry was a cover sell trade and came at around 15600 levels in Sep 2009. It is denoted by the first down arrow in the above chart. You will notice that in this chart, the price quickly moved in the opposite direction and you could use the break in the pivotal high as an entry point for our third trade (and second buy trade) at around 15700 levels. The fourth entry was a cover sell trade and came at around 17300 levels in Dec 2009. It is denoted by the second down arrow in the above chart. We keep repeating the same rules for the fifth (third up arrow in the above chart) and sixth trade (third down arrow in the above chart) as well.

Stop loss levels at entry: The nearest pivotal high in the case of a sell trade and nearest pivotal low in the case of a buy trade are suitable stop loss levels.

Exit Point: As in all SAR trades, here too the exit for one trade becomes the entry for the next trade placed.

Apple price chart (monthly)

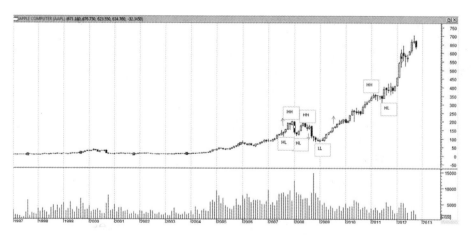

Fig 3.17

Entry points: The first entry was a buy trade and came in around 8 USD levels in May 1998. It is denoted by the first up arrow in the above chart. You would have to keep raising your stops to the nearest pivotal low as this was a buy trade. The second entry was a cover sell trade and came at around 20 USD in Sep 2000. This is denoted by the first down arrow in the above chart. Your third trade (and second buy trade) would have been 9 USD levels in May 2003. The fourth entry was a sell trade and came at around 117 USD levels in Sep 2008. This is denoted by the second down arrow in the above chart. After the fourth entry, prices quickly reverse and another buy is generated at 193 USD levels due to a break in the nearest pivotal high. At 580 USD levels (as on July 2012), while this book is going into print, you would still be holding this trade, with trailing stops in place at the nearest pivotal lows.

Stop loss levels at entry: The nearest pivotal high in case of a sell trade and nearest pivotal lows in the case of a buy trade are suitable stop loss levels.

Exit Point: As in the case of SAR trades, here too the exit for one trade becomes the entry on the next trade.

Please note that it is very important to get in only when the trend changes from down to up or up to down and we have to wait patiently till that happens. It is never a great idea to either exit early after a trending move starts or to enter when the trend is already in place (as, for instance, in the case of Apple, the trending move started in October 2009 on the monthly charts). In such instances, remember what Alfred Marshall, who is considered to be one of the founders of economics, once said "The price of everything rises and falls from time to time and place to place". So wait till the opportunity presents itself.

IMPROVING THE PERFORMANCE OF PIVOT & COMPARATIVE ANALYSIS

> ## Choose the right timeframe

- According to back tests, pivots work best on a weekly timeframe for investors.

> ## Choose the right asset class

- Abstain from trading pivots for asset classes that are stuck in a trading range for a long time. Defensive stocks fall into this category.

- Performance of pivots vastly improves when applied to an asset class that has performed well with pivots in the past.

> ## Keep Filters

- Keep filters, if you are trading pivots on intra-day timeframes, to ensure that the break-outs from pivots are genuine. The below chart is a Nifty futures 15 minute timeframe chart and illustrates the benefit of having filters on intra-day timeframes.

Nifty futures (intra day)

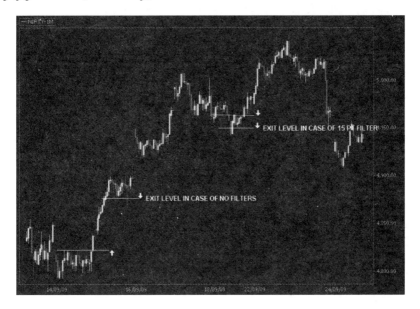

Fig 3.20

WHAT ARE FILTERS?

Filters helps you stay in a trade and be with a trend for a longer span, especially in case you are using pivots in intra-day timeframes. A filter is always kept below the nearest pivotal low in case of a buy trade and above nearest pivotal high in the case of a sell trade. For e.g., if the exit level for a buy trade according to a pivot is 5000, we will have 4985 as the buy cover area and vice-versa in case of a sell trade. In the above chart, the buy trade comes around 4825 levels. However, you would have covered the trade at 4875 since you had no filters. Since in this case you had filters, the exit came in at around 4950 only. Filters help us to stay in the trade when a false break out happens. Yet choosing the right filter level (in this case study we had a 15 point filter) is up to the trader of the asset class and must be done after testing the past performance with various filter levels.

PIVOT BACKTEST REPORT ON A DOW JONES (DJIA) WEEKLY TIMEFRAME

Back testing is done to test the performance of a set-up/pattern in the past. As price action is repetitive, a setup that has delivered a good performance in the past will have a high probability of succeeding in the future. Throughout this book, the emphasis will be on patterns and set-ups that have scored high on back tested performances. It is critical in real-time trading to trade based on the evidence we have on hand and that evidence is provided by back test reports. We will also have a higher level of confidence while placing trades when we know that a pattern/set up works and this confidence will have a positive impact on the way we trade.

Below is a DJIA weekly chart which forms the basis of trades suggested in the table (Fig.3.22) also called the back test sheet that follows.

DJIA (weekly)

Fig 3.21

While back testing pivots, the rule that we followed was Stop and Reverse (SAR) which means when we exit a sell trade, we not only square up our existing trade but place a fresh buy order as well and vice-versa. This ensures we are always in the market and with its current flow. All the entries made on the back test sheet will show where we would have entered and at what point we would have exited based on the set up we followed. The below sheet is the back test sheet of DJIA with the SAR rule followed from June 2002 to Jan 2010. As we can see from the sheet, if we followed the pivot rules, we would have made 6,225 points on the Dow in 14 trades. The last two trades are shown in the above DJIA weekly chart. The down arrow is the sell trade trigger on 27th June 08 and the up arrow is the buy trade trigger on 24th July 09.

The exit for the last trade was taken as 10328, which was the closing price of the Dow on 1st Jan 2010

DJIA trades

Trades	weekly DJIA Date	Buy/Sell	Entry	Exit	Profit/Loss
1	07-06-2002	S	9787	8087	1700
2	21-03-2003	B	8087	10009	1922
3	14-05-2004	S	10009	10365	-356
4	05-11-2004	B	10365	10365	0
5	15-04-2005	S	10365	10663	-298
6	22-07-2004	B	10663	11037	374
7	09-06-2006	S	11037	11273	-236
8	04-08-2006	B	11273	13252	1979
9	03-08-2007	S	13252	14020	-768
10	05-10-2007	B	14020	12722	-1298
11	11-01-2008	S	12722	12777	-55
12	18-04-2008	B	12777	11743	-1034
13	27-06-2008	S	11743	8888	2855
14	24-07-2009	B	8888	10328	1440
				TOTAL	6225

Fig 3.22

PIVOT BACKTEST REPORT ON EUR/USD WEEKLY CHARTS

Here's another example of back testing using a Weekly frequency Eur/USD Chart with Buy and Sell signals. The basis for the signals is pivots.

Euro/USD (weekly)

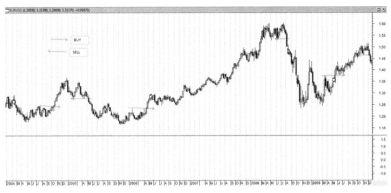

Fig 3.23

On pivot trades in the EUR/USD weekly charts, we had just 6 trading opportunities from October 2004 to February 2010.

Between the Dow Jones and EUR/USD, pivot-based trades can be implemented in EUR/USD as pivots have delivered more profitable trades and fewer negative trades (in fact they have had no negative trades) during the time period used for comparison.

Euro/USD trades

EUR/USD WEEKLY from 2nd Oct 2004 - 6th February 2010				
Date	Buy/Sell	Entry	Exit	Profit/Loss
10-02-2004	buy	1.2388	1.2758	0.037
14-05-2005	sell	1.2758	1.2308	0.045
03-09-2005	buy	1.2308	1.5381	0.3073
24-09-2005	sell	1.5381	1.3740	0.1641
22-05-2006	buy	1.3740	1.4616	0.0876
09-08-2008	sell	1.4616	1.3628	0.0988
			TOTAL	0.7398
1.3628 was the closing as on 6th Feb 2010				

Fig 3.24

Exercises

Pivots – Using the Dow Theory to Trade

1) *What is the long-term underlying trend in the Nikkei 225 price chart ?*

A)   Uptrend

B)   Downtrend

C)   Sideways

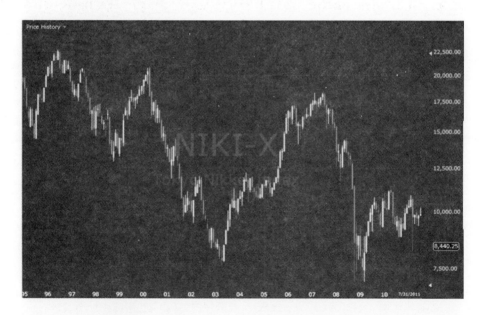

Answer: We can spot a series of lower highs and lower lows in the charts and hence the long-term trend is down.

TECHNICAL ANALYSIS

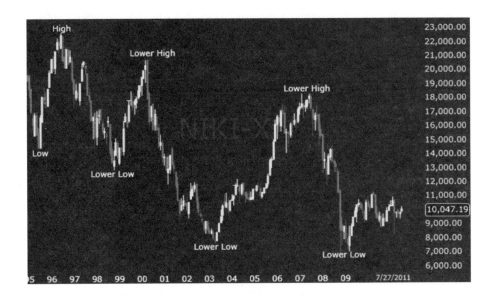

2) *How many Higher Lows are visible in the chart below?*

A) One

B) Three

C) None

3) *Can you spot any trend change ?*

A) There is no trend change in the chart

B) Downtrend spotted when the Higher low was broken

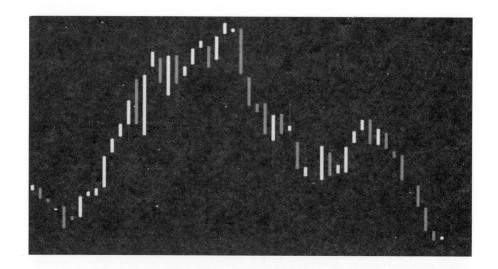

Answer: There were three higher lows spotted in the chart (marked as HL 1, HL 2 and HL 3) and the Trend Change was spotted when the Higher low (HL 3) was broken on the downside.

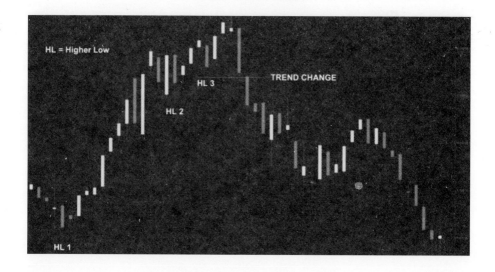

TECHNICAL ANALYSIS

4) *Mark the entry, stop-loss and exit levels for all the buy entries in the HDFC Weekly charts below.*

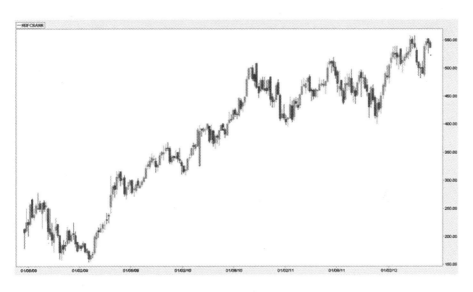

Answer: There were three buy entries in the charts. These are marked with up arrows. The stop-loss levels are marked by a horizontal line for each entry and the exit areas for each buy entry are marked by down arrows in the chart.

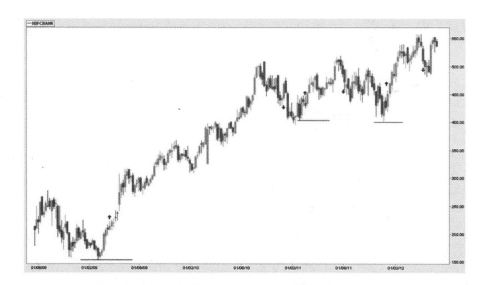

5)   Using Pivots , find the buy areas (with stop-losses) and exit areas in the Gold monthly charts below.

TECHNICAL ANALYSIS

Answer: There were only 2 buy signals in the Gold monthly charts since 1999 while one buy entry came at approximately USD 350, with an exit at approximately USD 800, you would still be holding the second buy entry which came at USD 1000. Since we are analyzing long-term trends, log charts are used. In the chart below, the up arrow denotes buy areas and the line denotes stop-loss levels while exit areas are denoted by down arrows. Since we haven't exited from the second buy entry, no exit area is marked.

ABOUT GAPS

CHAPTER 4

Overview with rules

*G*aps represent areas in a price chart where no trading takes place. The Gap where the current period's low is higher than the previous period's high is called a Gap-Up and vice-versa for a Gap-Down. **Any gap on a price chart can be divided into two types: Minor gaps and visual gaps.** While visual gaps are also called major gaps, minor gaps are also called common gaps.

Minor gaps are those gaps that are not visible to the naked eye and visual gaps represent those gaps that are visible and prominent on price charts. *Both visual gaps and minor gaps frequent price charts but visual gaps provide trading opportunities while minor gaps do not.*

Goldman Sachs intra day chart

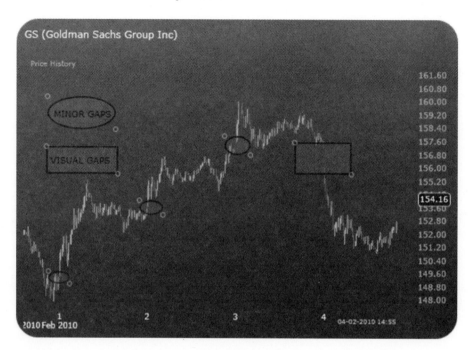

Fig 4.1

In the above chart, there are four gaps

TECHNICAL ANALYSIS

Intel Corp intra day chart

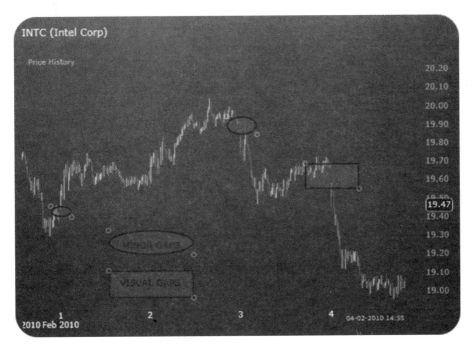

Fig 4.2

The first two gaps in the above chart are minor gaps while the last one is a Visual gap.

Visual gaps are also called by different names depending upon where they appear on the price charts. Visual gaps that are preceded by a price congestion or a technical pattern are called break-away gaps. Runaway gaps are visual gaps that help us to set a target as they occur about halfway through an up or down move. In such cases, we can expect prices to move about the same extent from the gap to the end of the move (a congestion or reversal pattern) as they have from the beginning of the move to the gap. A run-away gap is an indicator of a strong underlying trend. The final visual gap that reverses the trending move is called an exhaustion gap.

Mini Nifty chart

Fig 4.3

As visible from the Minifty chart, the breakaway gap was preceded by a V spike. We have to act conservatively in a situation wherein we see more than two runaway gaps, as each successive runaway gap brings us nearer to a price top or bottom.

The gap that reverses the trending move is called an exhaustion gap. It is very difficult to distinguish it from a runaway gap until the pattern is complete. An exhaustion gap, as illustrated in the case study, is usually accompanied by a day of relatively very high trading volumes. Exhaustion gaps are usually filled within 5 days and indicate a change in trend.

Case study: Nifty futures

The below Nifty futures daily timeframe chart provides an illustration

TECHNICAL ANALYSIS

of how a runaway gap can be used to measure the magnitude of the future trend. The distance from the lowest price point in the rally up to the first runaway gap (which occurred on May 4th 2009) was 1300 points (2300 to 3600) and Nifty futures achieved the target of 1300 points (from 3600 to 4900) within the next few months.

Nifty futures chart

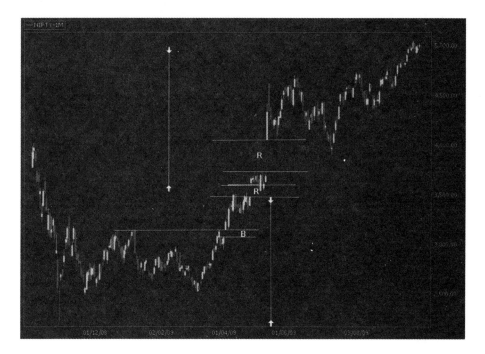

Fig 4.4

TRADING WITH VISUAL GAPS

"BUY WHEN PRICE MAKES A VISUAL GAP BAR HIGH, SELL WHEN PRICE MAKES A VISUAL GAP BAR LOW"

Goldman Sachs intra day chart

Fig 4.5

Entry point: On 7th June 2012, we see a Visual Gap up bar and we wait for the price to break in any direction. In this case, the entry will be on the sell side at 96 USD levels, since the price breaks the lowest point of the Visual Gap bar. If the Gap high is breached then we would have entered on the buy side.

Stop loss levels at entry: The highest price point of the Gap bar which is 97.5 will be the stop loss for this trade.

Exit Point: When the trend changes as per pivot rules, it is time to exit. In this case, the trend changed to up around 94.2 USD levels on the same day. Undertaking SAR trades, i.e. the exit for one trade becomes the entry on the next trade, applies here as well.

Note: The sell point depends on the timeframe we are trading in. If we are trading using a daily timeframe, we should take the low of the day and see if the low is breached in the days to follow. If we are trading the 15 min timeframe, we take the low on the first 15 minute candle and wait for the low to be breached before we place a sell side trade. Likewise, if the high of a visual gap bar is breached, then we will trade long with a stop loss set at the period low with a pivot break as the target. *Our target for any trade based on visual gaps will always be a pivot break.*

Accenture intra day chart

Fig 4.6

Entry point: On 6th June 2012, we see a visual gap up bar and we wait for the price to break in any direction. In this case, the entry will be on the buy side at 58 USD levels since the price breaks the highest point of the visual gap bar. If the gap low had been breached, we would have entered on the sell side.

Stop loss levels at entry: The low point of the gap bar, which is 57.15, will be the stop loss for this trade.

Exit Point: In this case, we will not wait till the trend changes, according to pivot rules, as another gap bar was spotted the following day. Since the gap low was broken, we would have exited the trade at 59 USD.

Hence the exit for any trade entered into based on visual gaps will be the pivot break or visual gap break, whichever occurs earlier, in the opposite direction of the original trade.

General Electric intra day chart

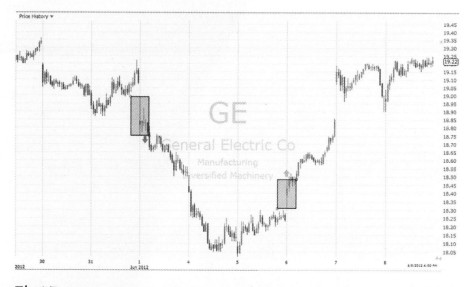

Fig 4.7

TECHNICAL ANALYSIS

Entry points: We have two trading opportunities on the chart. On 1st June 2012, we have a visual gap up bar and we wait for the price to break in any direction. In this case, the entry will be on the sell side at 18.75 USD levels, since the price breaks the lowest point of the visual gap bar. Then, on 6th June 2012, we have the next entry. This time it is on the buy side as the visual gap bar was breached on the higher side.

Stop loss levels at entry: The highest price point of the Gap bar which is 19USD will be the stop loss for the first trade. For the June 6th 2012 trade the lowest point of the Visual Gap bar will be the stop loss area.

Exit Point: The exit point for a visual gap trade, as mentioned earlier, will be when the trend changes as per pivot rules or when another visual gap emerges, whichever occurs earlier. In the case of the first trade, the exit was triggered at 18.25 USD, on the 5thJune 2012. For the second trade, the exit could be on 7th June 2012, i.e., when the Visual Gap bar low was breached.

Case study: Deutsche bank (Daily timeframe)

In the chart below, we can sell below the low of the visual gap bar and cover when the pivot triggers a trend change.

Deutsche Bank chart

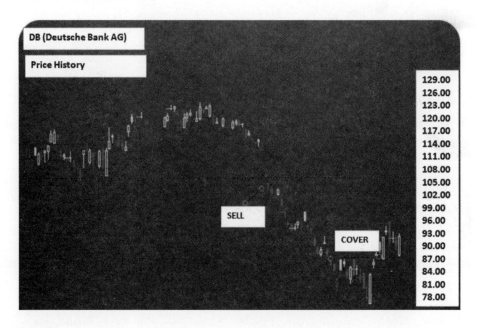

Fig 4.8

Entry point: Towards late May 2008, we see a break below the visual gap bar around 105 USD. While we have several gap areas on the chart, only one gap can be categorized as a visual gap as its very easy to spot with the naked eye.

Stop loss levels at entry: The highest price point of the gap bar, which is 108 USD, will be the stop loss for the trade.

TECHNICAL ANALYSIS

Exit Point: The exit point for this trade will be the pivot break which occurs around 90 USD levels.

COMBINING PIVOTS WITH VISUAL GAP TRADES

Nifty futures intra day chart

Fig 4.9

Figure 4.9 is a case study which shows how to trade based on pivots and visual gap signals using Stop And Reverse (SAR as detailed in the previous chapter on pivots), from 29th January 2010 to 9th February 2010. Up arrows in the chart represent the buy levels and down arrows are sell levels. In the above chart, all the horizontal lines represent the stop loss levels for the last buy signal (the last up arrow in the above chart). We can also see that the trail stop levels keep rising as we adjust our SAR level to the nearest higher bottom.

Why do we have filters in visual gap trades?

As we understood the importance of filters while trading using Pivots, it is important to have filters for visual gap trades as well.

In the Credit Suisse chart below, we can see a visual gap and hence we would like to place a buy order above the high of the opening bar. However, the bears have other plans as they push prices down. Now, if we had a filter, the buy would not have been triggered. Instead, we would have been on the sell side as price breaches the low of the bar and would have held on to the trade till the pivot triggers an uptrend.

Credit Suisse chart

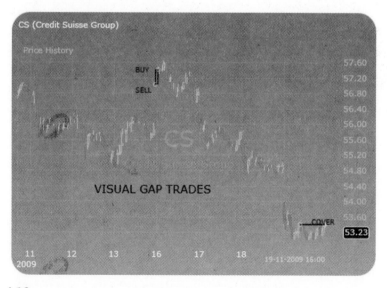

Fig 4.10

TECHNICAL ANALYSIS

Integrating pivot trades with visual gap trade makes for an exciting trading system. However, we should keep in mind:

If we were holding buy positions based on pivots and we have a visual gap (up or down) during the day, we should wait for the period low (filter incase of intra-day timeframes) to be breached before entering the sell side and reversing our buys. Vice-versa also applies for sell positions entered, based on pivots.

Case study: Nifty futures (15 minutes timeframe)

In the Fig 4.11, B stands for Buy and C stands for Cover. The initial trade was a buy order as the price breaks through the high of the gap candle (we had a 10 point filter for the below trade). Hence even though the price broke through the low of the candle, we don't sell as our 10 point filter was not breached. This initial buy is covered when a pivot triggers a downtrend and breaches our filters as well.

Nifty futures intra day chart

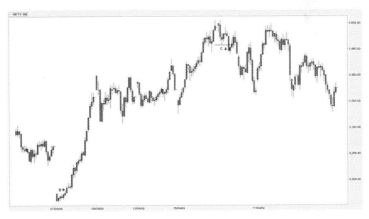

Fig 4.11

To recap, pivots combined with gap trades can provide good results and allow us to follow the market and stay with the trend till the direction changes.

Exercises

About GAPS

1)   *Name the Gap which reverses a trending move?*

A)   Exhaustion

B)   Run-away

C)   Break-away

Answer: A

2)   *What should be the target for a trade entered based on Visual Gaps?*

A)   We should hold the trade till the next visual Gap

B)   We have to exit when Pivot Breaks in the direction opposite to the original entry

C)   When we spot exhaustion gap we should exit the trade

Answer: B

3) *Circle the Visual Gaps you can spot in the 15 minute intra-day charts of Ford Motors.*

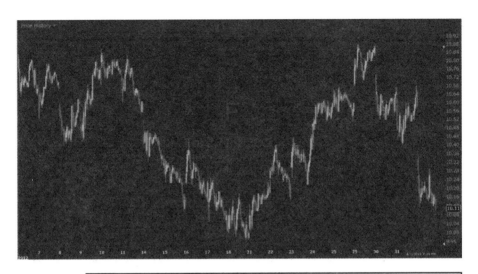

Answer: There were five visual gaps on the charts circled as below.

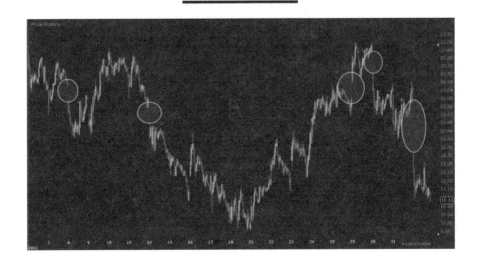

4) *Mark the entry and exit levels for all the visual gaps in the IBM Intra-day chart below?*

Answer:

There were three visual gaps in the charts. The first gap signaled a sell trigger, while the second and third were buy triggers. All stop loss areas are shown in the chart by lines near the entry area.

TECHNICAL ANALYSIS

TOPS AND BOTTOMS

CHAPTER 5

About double top and double bottom

A double top is a bearish set-up and develops when the price formation forms two consecutive peaks of a similar height. The prices move up to a certain level, face resistance and then moves down. Then again demand comes in and pushes prices higher and again the move gets resisted at the same level. However, the second time around, due to a higher supply pressure, prices don't find any support and hence a breakout occurs, pushing prices even lower. The converse is true with double bottoms, wherein demand gets the better of supply and this results in a breakout which pushes prices even lower. As visible in Fig 5.1, a double top looks like the letter 'M'. Similarly, a double bottom looks like a 'W'.

Double Top

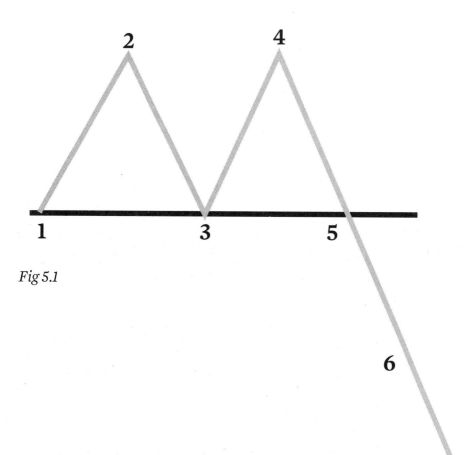

Fig 5.1

RULES TO RECOGNIZE DOUBLE TOPs:

A double top formation conforms to the following sequence:

→ In Fig 5.1, Point 2 is the reaction high of point 1

→ Point 3 is the reaction low of point 2 (noted that point 1 and point 3 are at equal levels)

→ Point 4 is the reaction high of point 3 (noted that point 4 and point 2 are at approximately equal levels)

→ Point 5 is the point where the extended trend line that connects point 1 and point 3 breaks. In other words point 5 is the breakout point.

SIGNIFICANCE OF VARIOUS POINTS IN A DOUBLE TOP SET UP:

→ Point 1 may either be a period low or a pivot or any point in a period bar

→ Point 5 is the sell point

→ Point 4 is the stop-loss point

And your target (i.e. how many points below your entry point you plan to exit) is the distance between point 4 and point 5. So, for instance, if the distance between point 4 and point 5 is 20, then the buy point for the asset class is 20 points below 5. In other words, point 5 is the mid-point between point 4 and the target area (point 6 in the above image).

IBM price chart (weekly)

Fig 5.2

Pattern: Double Top

Entry point: The entry level was around 116 USD (Point 5 in the above chart). The entry was by way of a sell trade.

Stop loss levels at entry: Around 130 USD (Point 4 in the above chart) would be a good place to place a stop loss.

Exit Point: The exit level for the trade will be around 102 USD levels. We arrive at this exit point by marking the distance between point 4 and 5, which is 14 USD and then applying it to our entry level, i.e.116 – 14 = 102 (since the exit will be in the form of a buy to cover our entry in the form of a sell trade).

In the above example, you can clearly discern the letter M on the charts and point 2 and point 4 are approximately at equal levels. You will also notice that the entry level was apparent from a break in the pivot level (when point 3 was broken on the downside).

Double Bottom

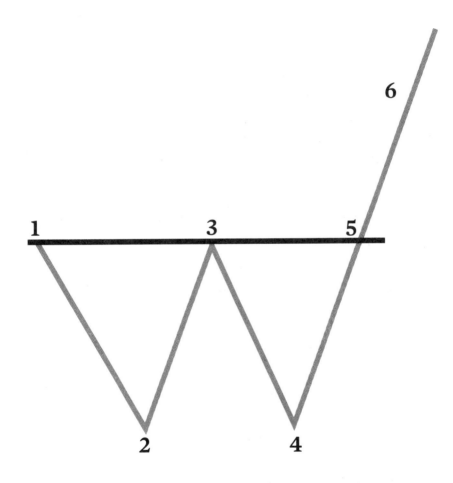

Fig 5.3

RULES TO RECOGNIZE DOUBLE BOTTOMs:

A double bottom formation conforms to the following sequence:

→ In the Fig 5.3, Point 2 is the reaction low of point 1

→ Point 3 is the reaction high of point 2 (point 1 and point 3 are at equal levels)

→ Point 4 is the reaction low of point 3 (point 4 and point 2 are at approximately equal levels)

→ Point 5 is the point where the extended trend line that connects point 1 and point 3 breaks. In other words point 5 is the breakout point.

SIGNIFICANCE OF VARIOUS POINTS IN A DOUBLE BOTTOM SET UP:

Point 1 may either be a period high or a pivot or any point in a period bar.

→ Point 5 is the buy point

→ Point 4 is the stop-loss point

→ And your target (i.e. how many points below your entry point you plan to exit) is the distance between point 4 and point 5. For instance, if the distance between point 4 and point 5 is 20, then the target for the asset class is point 5 20 points above 5.

TECHNICAL ANALYSIS

In other words, point 5 is the mid-point between point 4 and the target area (point 6 in the above image).

World Gold Index (monthly)

Fig 5.4

Pattern: Double Bottom

Entry point: The entry level was around 350 USD (Point 5 in the above chart) in the form of a buy trade.

Stop loss levels at entry: Around 250 USD (Point 4 in the above chart) would be a good point to set a stop loss.

Exit Point: Since the distance between point 4 and 5 is 100 USD, the exit level for the trade will be around 450 USD levels. Effectively, it will be 100 USD above the entry level of 350 USD in the form of a sell trade.

In the above chart, the letter W is visible and point 2 and point 4 are approximately at equal levels. The entry level was apparent due to a break in the pivot level (when point 3 was broken on the upside).

This pattern, which took about 6 years to form, marked a long consolidation in Gold charts and took Gold prices to a new all-time high of about 1900 USD over the next 8 years.

Case Study charts for Double Top and Double Bottom Set-ups

Euro/USD (daily)

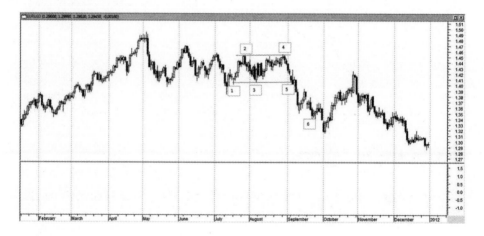

Fig 5.5

Pattern: Double Top

Entry point: The entry level was around 140 (Point 5 in the above chart) in the form of a sell trade.

TECHNICAL ANALYSIS

Stop loss levels at entry: Around 145 (Point 4 in the above chart) would be a good point to place a stop loss.

Exit Point: The exit level for the trade will be around 135 levels (since the distance between point 4 and 5 is 5 USD, the exit level should be 5 USD below the entry level of 140) in the form of a buy trade to cover out initial sell.

Nifty (weekly)

Fig 5.6

Pattern: Double Bottom

Entry point: The entry level was around 1100 (Point 5 in the above chart) in the form of a buy trade.

Stop loss levels at entry: Around 920 (Point 4 in the above chart) would be a good point to place a stop loss.

Exit Point: The exit level for the trade will be around 1280 levels (since the distance between point 4 and 5 is 180, the exit level will be 180 points above the entry level of 1100) in the form of a sell trade to cover our initial buy.

This pattern, which took about a year (between June 2002 to June 2003) to form, marked a period of consolidation in the Nifty charts and after the breakout the Nifty went to a new all-time high of about 6300 in January 2008.

Reliance price chart (daily)

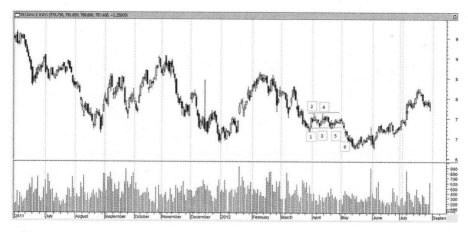

Fig 5.7

Pattern: Double Top

Entry point: The entry level was around 725 (Point 5 in the above chart) in the form of a sell trade.

Stop loss levels at entry: A stop loss can be set at around 760 (Point

4 in the above chart).

Exit Point: The exit level for the trade will be around 690 levels (since the distance between point 4 and 5 is 35, the exit level should be 35 Rupees below the entry level of 725) in the form of a buy trade to cover our initial sell.

The entry was warranted at Rs 725 but after the entry the stock did not go down immediately. It consolidated for a while before heading towards the target area. So it's important to be patient and wait either till the target is achieved or the stop loss is triggered before exiting from a trade.

DJIA (quarterly)

Fig 5.8

Pattern: Double Bottom

Entry point: The entry level was around 160 (Point 5 in the above chart) in the form of a buy trade.

Stop loss levels at entry: A stop loss can be placed around 92 (Point 4 in the above chart).

Exit Point: The exit level for the trade should be around 228 levels (since the distance between point 4 and 5 is 68, the exit level will be 68 points above the entry level of 160) in the form of a sell trade to cover our initial buy.

This pattern appeared after the great depression of the 1930's which saw the Dow crash 90% in a span of 3 years, from a high of 386 in September 1929 to merely 40 points in September 1932. This crash was followed by a pull-back rally and later by a period of consolidation, which saw the double bottom pattern emerge. After the breakout from this pattern, the Dow Jones started its relentless march upwards.

Crude oil (daily)

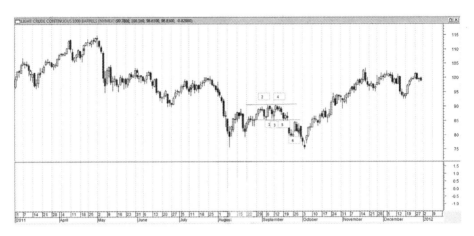

Fig 5.9

Pattern: Double Top

Entry point: The entry level was around 85 USD (Point 5 in the above chart) in the form of a sell trade.

Stop loss levels at entry: A stop loss could be set at around 90 USD (Point 4 in the above chart).

Exit Point: The exit level for the trade should be around 80 levels (since the distance between point 4 and 5 is 5 USD, the exit level will be 5 USD below the entry level of 85) in the form of a buy trade to cover our initial sell.

The chart shows a downtrend in crude prices starting April 2011 and the pattern break out takes place in the direction of the pre-existing trend. So, the key message is that Double top and bottom patterns can take place in either the direction of the trend or reverse the trend (from down to up or up to down).

HDFC Bank price chart (weekly)

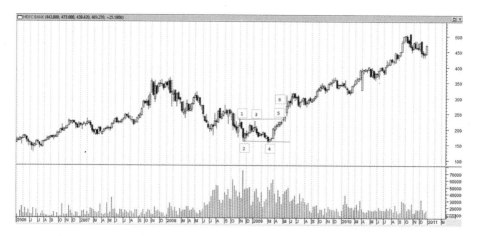

Fig 5.10

Pattern: Double Bottom

Entry point: The entry level was around Rs 230(Point 5 in the above chart) in the form of a buy trade.

Stop loss levels at entry: The stop loss could be set at around Rs 160 (Point 4 in the above chart).

Exit Point: The exit level for the trade will be around 300 levels (since the distance between point 4 and 5 which is Rs 70, the exit level will be Rs 70 above the entry level of Rs 230) in the form of a sell trade. The exit level is shown in the chart as point 6.

TECHNICAL ANALYSIS

The chart shows a downtrend in HDFC Bank's price starting from Jan 2008 and the pattern breakout took place against the direction of the pre-existing trend. However after the breakout in Apr 2009, the stock has had a great upswing in prices. One of the flip sides of having a target based trade is that there is a possibility that you may exit early and miss out on a great trending move, as in the case study above and in some of the case studies earlier in this section as well.

So far we saw the most powerful of all top and bottom patterns - double tops and bottoms. In the next section we will see other types of tops and bottoms, which are not as crucial to real time trading but could provide us with useful insights into the future direction of prices. Since rounding top/bottoms and triple tops/ bottoms are not high priority patterns, less emphasis has been laid on them in this book.

Rounding tops and bottoms

OVERVIEW

BULLISH SETUP

BEARISH SETUP

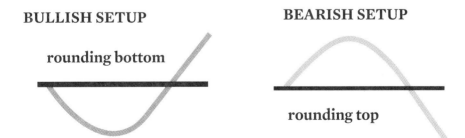

rounding bottom

rounding top

Fig 5.11

Also called saucers, as illustrated in Fig 5.11, rounding tops and bottoms form as a result of a very gradual shift in demand and supply. Once the highest point (in the case of rounding bottoms) and the lowest point (in case of rounding tops) is taken out, a breakout occurs, indicating a change in trend.

Unfortunately, rounding tops and bottoms don't have implications for measurement of trends i.e. we don't have any target and we only know a trend change has taken place.

Whenever a pattern doesn't have a target we consider pivot break as the target and hold on to the trade till the pivots trigger a change in trend.

World Silver Index (monthly)

Fig 5.12

TECHNICAL ANALYSIS

Pattern: Rounding Bottom

Entry point: The entry level was around 8 USD (marked with an up arrow in the charts) in the form of a buy trade.

Stop loss levels at entry: A stop loss can be set at around 4 USD which is the lowest point of the consolidation area in the charts.

Exit Point: The exit level for the trade will be around 16 USD levels which is the pivot break after the entry was triggered on the charts.

The chart shows a consolidation which started in 1998 and continued until 2004. After the entry was triggered, there was a brief period during which prices went down. After that the uptrend started gaining strength. We need to look for a break in a major pivotal area for a rounding bottom pattern (in Fig 5.12, the major pivotal high was observed in 1998 and the uptick in prices started only after it was broken in 2004.

Crude oil (weekly)

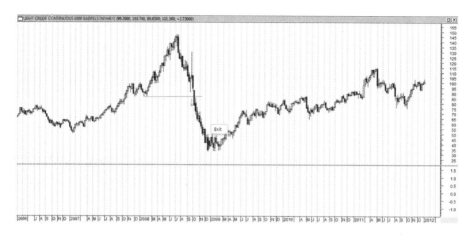

Fig 5.13

Pattern: Rounding Top

Entry point: The entry level was around USD 85 (marked with a down arrow in the charts) in the form of a sell trade.

Stop loss levels at entry: The stop loss could be set at around USD 145 as it the highest point of the consolidation area in the charts.

Exit Point: The exit level for the trade will be around USD 49 levels which is the pivot break after the entry was triggered on the charts.

This chart shows a period of accumulation, which started in 2007 and peaked in July 2008. However after that supply gradually picked up and prices started to move down especially after the rounding top pattern triggered a sell at USD 85 levels. Also noted that the entry was at USD 85 while the stop loss area is at 145, i.e. there is a difference of about 60 USD which means the risk-return is not in our favour. Ideally, we should not enter trades in which the anticipated return is less than the risk we take. We should take only those trades where rewards are at least 2 times the risk taken (for e.g. if the stop loss, which represents risk, is Rs 60, the returns on the trade should be at least Rs 120).

TRIPLE TOPS AND BOTTOMS

OVERVIEW

The only difference between double tops and bottoms and triple tops and bottoms is that instead of two tops or two bottoms, triple tops/bottoms, as the name suggests, makes 3 tops/bottoms.

Triple tops and bottoms are extremely rare to find on higher timeframe charts (Weekly, Monthly and quarterly) and may sometimes form on intra-day timeframe charts. They are not patterns of high significance hence in-depth analysis is not required.

ACC price chart (intra day)

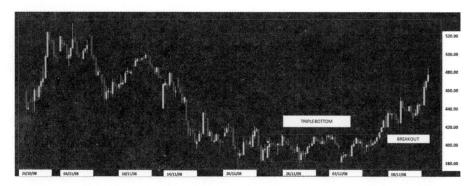

Fig 5.14

Pattern: Triple Bottom

Entry point: The entry level was around Rs 415 (marked with an up arrow in the charts) in the form of a buy trade.

Stop loss levels at entry: The stop loss was around Rs 385 as this is the lowest point of the triple bottom formation in the charts.

Exit Point: The exit level for the trade will be around Rs 455 (since the difference between the entry level and the stop loss level is Rs 40 and it is a buy trade, we add Rs 40 to the entry level to identify the exit area).

TECHNICAL ANALYSIS

Exercises

Tops and Bottoms

1) ***Double Top looks like ....***

A)   Letter Z

B)   Letter M

C)   Letter W

Answer: **B**

---

2) ***All the points in a double top or double bottom pattern are Pivotal points***

A)   No, some points in the pattern may not be pivotal

B)   Yes, all the points are pivotal points and the entry comes at a pivot break

C)   Yes, all the points are pivotal points however the entry to the trade may not always be due to pivot break

Answer: **B**

3) *Can you mark the double top and bottom patterns that are visible in the Dow Jones weekly chart below.*

Answer: There was one double top and one double bottom visible in the Dow Jones weekly chart. While the double top didn't achieve its target, the double bottom break out took Dow Jones to new highs.

4) *Do you spot any double top or bottom pattern in the IndusInd Bank weekly chart below?*

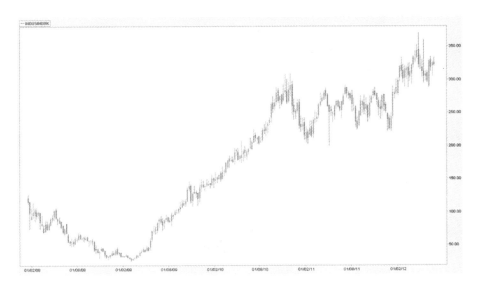

Answer: Yes, we can spot two double bottoms on the chart and both hit their respective targets. While the first double bottom reversed the trend in the charts from down to up, the second one occurred within the uptrend and also hit the target.

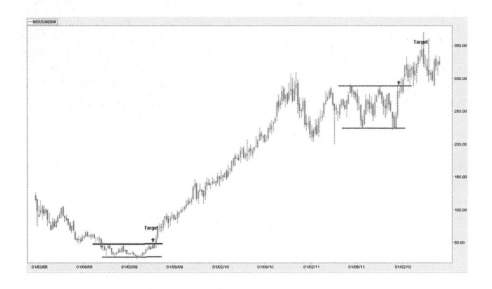

TECHNICAL ANALYSIS

5) *Do you spot any double top and bottom pattern in the below HDFC weekly chart ?*

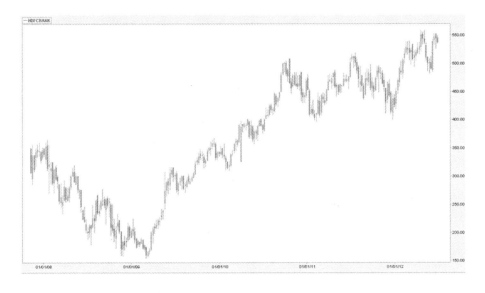

Answer:

Yes, we can spot one double bottom and one double top on the charts .While the double bottom hit the target, the double top moved towards the target but didn't hit it; the stop-loss was triggered. The key lesson here is that no trading system in the world gives 100% successful results. We will make losses along the way, learn to cope with them and move on to the next trade.

HEAD AND SHOULDERS

CHAPTER 6

About Head and Shoulders

O ne of the most widely followed patterns by technicians around the world is the head and shoulders (HS) set up. This pattern has two variants:

1. HS Top

2. HS Bottom OR Inverted HS

HS Tops with rules to recognize them

HS Tops has bearish implications and this pattern can act as both a reversal (of underlying trend) pattern or a continuation (of underlying trend) pattern.

Head and Shoulders Top

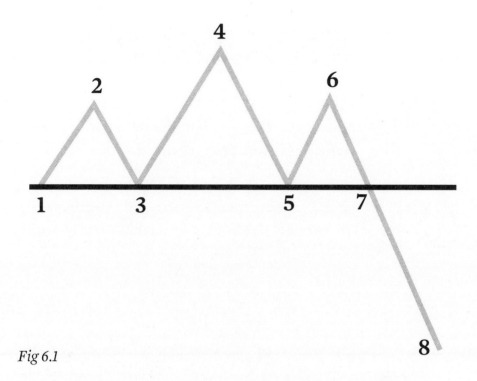

Fig 6.1

RULES TO RECOGNIZE HEAD AND SHOULDERS TOPs:

The Head and shoulders top formation conforms to the sequence that follows:

Point 2 is the reaction high of point 1

Point 3 is the reaction low of point 2

Point 4 is the reaction high of point 3 (point 4 is always higher than point 2) and none of the points are higher than point 4.

Point 5 is the reaction low of point 4

Point 6 is the reaction high of point 5 (point 6 is always lower than point 4)

Point 7 is the area where the trend line, that connects point 1, 3, and 5, breaks.

The trend line that connects point 1,3,5,and 7 is also called the neckline.

In any head and shoulders top pattern:

Point 1 may either be a period low or a pivot.

Point 7 is the sell point

Point 6 is the stop-loss point

And target is the distance between point 4 and point 7 for e.g. if the distance between point 4 and point 7 is 20, then the target for the asset class is point 7, i.e. 20 less than point 7

In other words, point 7 is the mid-point between point 4 and the target area (point 8 in Fig 6.1)

The rationale behind a Head & Shoulders top pattern is as follows:

1. ***Left Shoulder:*** Bulls push prices upwards, making new highs; however, bears begin to return and push prices slightly lower.

2. ***Head:*** The price takes out the high of the left shoulder but gains don't last long; soon the bears return and push prices lower.

3. ***Right Shoulder:*** The bulls push prices upward again, but this time fails to make a high. This is generally seen as a bearish sign as the bears do not allow the bulls to make a new high or even an equal high. The bears push prices back to the neckline (i.e. support line).

When price closes below the neckline, a sell signal is generated. A neckline is drawn across the bottom of the left shoulder, head and right shoulder. When the neckline is broken, we receive confirmation of a reversal in the trend. It is also possible to find that prices retest the neckline before continuing their downward march. Usually a downward sloping neckline is seen as a more powerful Head & Shoulders top pattern, mainly because a downward sloping neckline means that prices are making lower bottoms.

Now let's have a look at how the HS top pattern develops with the help of USD/CAD (Canadian Dollars) charts.

US/Cad chart

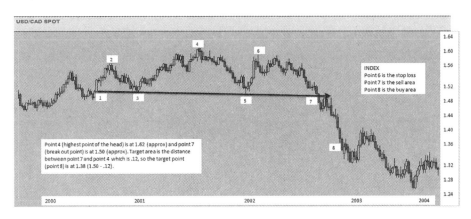

Fig 6.2

Head and Shoulders Bottom

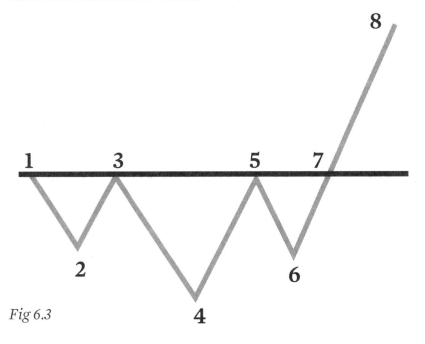

Fig 6.3

RULES TO RECOGNIZE HEAD AND SHOULDER BOTTOMs:

The head and shoulders bottom formation is simply the opposite of the head and shoulders top and conforms to the following sequence:

Point 2 is the reaction low of point 1

Point 3 is the reaction high of point 2

Point 4 is the reaction low of point 3 (noted that point 4 is always lower than point 2) and none of the points are lower than point 4.

Point 5 is the reaction high of point 4

Point 6 is the reaction low of point 5 (point 6 is always higher than point 4)

Point 7 is the area where the trend line that connects point 1, 3 and 5 breaks.

The trend line that connects points 1, 3, 5 and 7 is also called the neckline.

In any head and shoulders bottom pattern:

Point 1 may either be a period high or a pivot.

Point 7 is the buy point

Point 6 is the stop-loss point

And the target is the distance between point 4 and point 7. So, for example, if the distance between point 4 and point 7 is 20, then the target for the asset class is 20 above point 7.

In other words, point 7 is the mid-point between point 4 and the target area (point 8 in Fig 6.3).

The rationale behind a head and shoulders bottom pattern is as follows:

Head and shoulder bottoms (inverted head and shoulders) are simply the inverse of head and shoulder tops.

The HS bottom set up has bullish implications and this pattern can act as both a reversal pattern or a continuation pattern.

The rationale behind a Head & Shoulders bottom pattern is as follows:

➤   **Left Shoulder:** Bears push prices downwards, to make new lows; then bulls come in and push prices slightly higher.

➤   **Head:** Price gains don't last long as bears return and push prices even lower than before. Then prices find buyers at the new lower prices.

➤   **Right Shoulder:** The bears push downward again but this time they fail to make a lower low. This is generally seen as bullish sign because bulls do not allow the bears to make a new low or even an equal low. The bulls push prices back to the neckline (i.e. the resistance line).

When the price closes above the neckline, a buy signal is generated. A neckline is drawn across the top of the left shoulder, the head and the right shoulder. When the neckline is broken, we receive confirmation of a reversal in the trend. It is also possible to find that prices retest the neckline before continuing their upward march.

Usually an upward sloping neckline is seen as a more powerful Reverse Head & Shoulders pattern, mainly because an upward sloping neckline means that prices are making higher highs.

What's noteworthy about the inverted head and shoulders is the volume aspect. The inverted left shoulder should be accompanied by an increase in volume. The inverted head should be made with lighter volumes. The rally from the head however, should show greater volume than the rally from the left shoulder. Ultimately, the inverted right shoulder should register the lightest volume of all. When the market then rallies through the neckline, a big increase in volume should be seen.

GBP/US chart

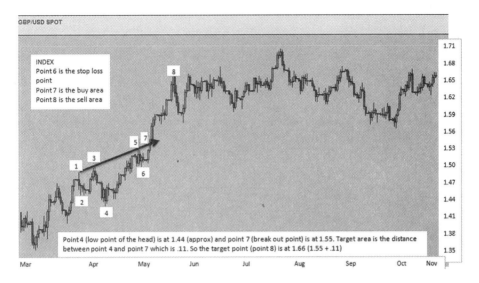

GBP/USD SPOT

INDEX
Point 6 is the stop loss
point
Point 7 is the buy area
Point 8 is the sell area

Point 4 (low point of the head) is at 1.44 (approx) and point 7 (break out point) is at 1.55. Target area is the distance between point 4 and point 7 which is .11. So the target point (point 8) is at 1.66 (1.55 + .11)

Fig 6.4

KEY POINTS

The neckline in the head and shoulders top and bottom patterns may be slanted upwards, downwards or sideways (as shown in the below images). However the slant of the neckline doesn't diminish its importance as one of the most reliable patterns which is less prone to false breakouts.

Head and Shoulders - Top and Bottom

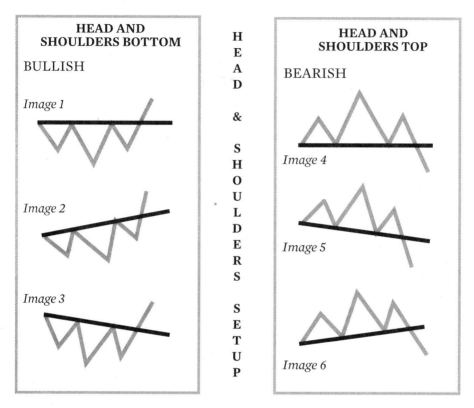

HEAD AND SHOULDERS BOTTOM

BULLISH

Image 1

Image 2

Image 3

HEAD & SHOULDERS SETUP

HEAD AND SHOULDERS TOP

BEARISH

Image 4

Image 5

Image 6

Fig 6.5

Usually with bearish patterns (i.e. patterns wherein a fall in prices is anticipated) volume doesn't play an important role as prices tend to fall on their own weight but with any bullish pattern (i.e. patterns wherein a rise in prices is anticipated) a breakout should always be accompanied by high volumes.

As with any technical analysis pattern, the larger the time frame the greater its importance i.e. **a pattern in a monthly chart carries**

greater significance than a pattern in a five minute or an hourly chart.

Case Study charts for Head and shoulders Top and Bottom

Silver chart (daily)

Fig 6.6

Entry point: The entry level was around USD 40.5 (point 7 in the charts) in the form of a sell trade.

Stop loss levels at entry: A stop loss can be set at around USD 43.5, which is the highest point of the right shoulder (point 6 in the charts).

Exit Point: The exit level for the trade will be around USD 36 levels (since the difference between point 4 and point 7 is USD 4 and it's a sell trade, we subtract USD 4 to the entry level to identify the exit area).

Hindustan Unilever price chart (weekly)

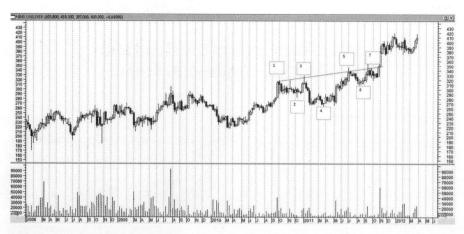

Fig 6.7

Pattern: Head and Shoulders Bottom

Entry point: The entry level was around Rs 350 (point 7 in the charts) in the form of a buy trade.

Stop loss levels at entry: A stop loss can be set at around Rs 300, which is the lowest point of the right shoulder (point 6 in the charts).

Exit Point: The exit level for the trade will be around Rs 450 (since the difference between point 4 and point 7 is Rs 100 and it's a buy trade, we add Rs 100 to the entry level to identify the exit area).

TECHNICAL ANALYSIS

Euro/USD chart (daily)

Fig 6.8

Pattern: Head and Shoulders Top

Entry point: The entry level was around 1.31 (point 7 in the charts) in the form of a sell trade.

Stop loss levels at entry: The stop loss was around 1.34, which is the highest point of the right shoulder (point 6 in the charts).

Exit Point: The exit level for the trade will be around 1.27 (Since the difference between point 4 and point 7 is 0.4 and it's a sell trade, we subtract 0.4 from the entry level to identify the exit area).

S&P chart (quarterly)

Fig 6.9

Pattern: Head and Shoulders Bottom

Entry point: The entry level was around 150 (point 7 in the charts) in the form of a buy trade.

Stop loss levels at entry: Stop loss for this trade will be around 100, which is the lowest point of the right shoulder (point 6 in the charts).

Exit Point: The exit level for the trade will be around 240 (Since the difference between point 4 and point 7 is 90 and it's a buy trade, we add 90 to the entry level to identify the exit area).

SPX was within an area of consolidation between 1969 and 1983 when the head and shoulders pattern was formed. After the breakout from the pattern, SPX entered a new bull phase and reached new highs consistently. The SPX is the world's most widely traded derivatives index.

Ford price chart (intra day)

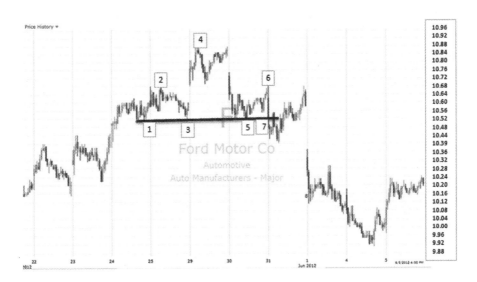

Fig 6.10

Pattern: Head and Shoulders Top

Entry point: The entry level was around USD 10.5 (point 7 in the charts) in the form of a sell trade.

Stop loss levels at entry: Stop loss for this trade will be around USD 10.7, which is the highest point of the right shoulder (point 6 in the charts).

Exit Point: The exit level for the trade will be around USD 10.15 (Since the difference between point 4 and point 7 is 0.35 and it's a buy trade, we subtract 0.35 to the entry level to identify the exit area).

After the entry was made at USD 10.5 levels, the prices retraced back to the right shoulder high but didn't go above it. Hence from a trade management perspective, it is always prudent to place stop loss trades a few ticks above/below the shoulder high/low, depending upon whether we are trading a head and shoulders top or bottom. For instance, in the above example we should place a stop loss at USD 10.75.

Nifty chart (daily)

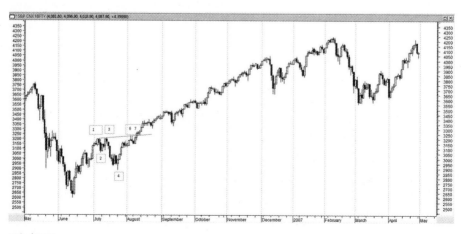

Fig 6.11

TECHNICAL ANALYSIS

Entry point: The entry level was around 3200 (point 7 in the charts) in the form of a buy trade.

Stop loss levels at entry: The stop loss for this trade will be around 3000, which is the lowest point of the right shoulder (point 6 in the charts).

Exit Point: The exit level for the trade will be around 3550 (Since the difference between point 4 and point 7 is 350 and it's a buy trade, we add 350 to the entry level to identify the exit area).

Exercises

Head and Shoulders

1) *A buy signal is generated by the head and shoulders bottom pattern when the*

A) Price closes above the neckline

B) Price closes below the neckline

Answer: $\boxed{A}$

2) *How do you measure the target for a head and shoulders top pattern?*

A) The target is the lowest point of the pattern to the neckline

B) The target is measured as the distance from the top of the head and the neckline

C) The target will be the distance from the right shoulder and the neckline

Answer: **B**

3) *Do you spot any Head and Shoulders pattern in the below CBOE-VIX weekly chart ?*

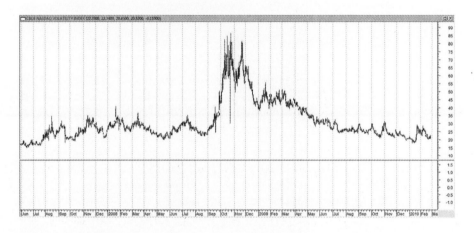

Answer: There was a bullish head and shoulders on the charts which hit the target point (8 in the below charts) in the same week. Also it's important to spot the patterns with the naked eye without drawing trendlines and though it's difficult when you begin, once you gain experience it will be easier.

5) ***Can you spot any Head and Shoulders pattern in the Citibank weekly charts below?***

TECHNICAL ANALYSIS

Answer: There was a Head and Shoulders top which was spotted on the chart which achieved the target easily. The long-term uptrend on the Citibank chart was also broken and the downtrend was triggered by this pattern, which saw Citibank shares plunging from a high of USD 570 in December 2006 to a low of USD 9.70 in March 2009

IRREGULAR DIAGONALS

CHAPTER 7

About Irregular Diagonals

*I*rregular diagonals develop either when the preceding move has gone "too far too fast" or as a continuation to a larger trend move. In most cases, they either indicate exhaustion and tell us that a fast move in the opposite direction is on the horizon or alert us to a fast paced move in the direction of the underlying trend after a consolidation. The key point to note is that the movement after the pattern triggers a trade will be fast.

The term 'Diagonals' is also used in the Elliott wave theory for what is commonly referred as a wedge pattern (this will be discussed in a later chapter). Irregular diagonals, which we are discussing here look similar to diagonals/wedges, except for the irregular point 5.

Irregular Diagonals

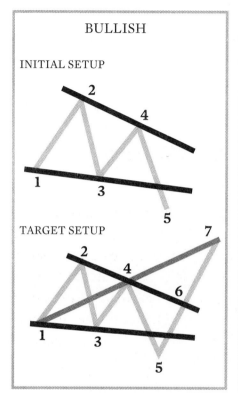
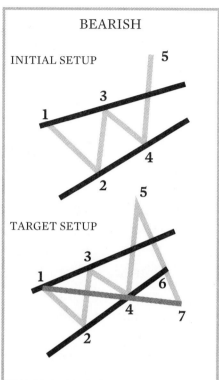

Fig 7.1

'Irregular diagonals' are patterns that help us trade the false breakouts that may occur in some setups, with specific target levels. Irregular diagonal patterns consist of 5 points. Within these, points 1 – 4 are always pivots, while point 5 is an irregular wave that stretches beyond the trendline connecting points 1 – 3. The target area (point 6) is an extension of the trend line that connects point 1 and point 4.

TECHNICAL ANALYSIS

In a bullish irregular diagonal, bears enter fresh positions believing that a fresh breakout has taken place on the downside. This is due to their observation that the trendline 1 – 3 breaks on the downside and is accompanied by a fresh pivot break, indicating selling pressure. At this stage, the market is oversold and even a small amount of buying pushes prices up as people who should sell have already sold and the market is only left with buyers. This alone is enough for prices to move up at a rapid pace and reach the target price (i.e the line 1-7 in the above image). The opposite is true in case of bearish irregular diagonals.

The initial set-up and the target set-up for irregular diagonals looks like the above image. Also note that the bearish irregular diagonal pattern always slopes up while a bullish irregular diagonal pattern always slopes down.

Bearish Irregular Diagonal

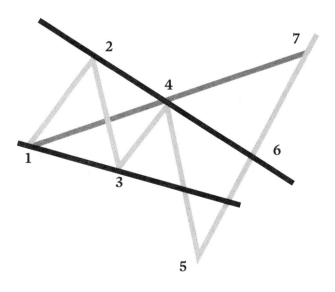

Fig 7.2

RULES TO RECOGNIZE BULLISH IRREGULAR DIAGONALS:

In any irregular diagonal pattern, point 1 is always a pivot.

Point 2 is the reaction high of point 1

Point 3 is the reaction low of point 2 and point 3 will always be lower than point 1

Point 4 is the reaction high of point 3 and point 4 is always lower than point 2

Point 5 is an irregular point that extends below the trend line that connects point 1 and point 3

Point 5 is also the stop loss point.

Point 6 is the buy point which is an extension of the trend line that connects point 2 and point 4.

Point 7 is the target point and is the extension of trend line that connects point 1 and point 4.

While trading on irregular diagonals, the trend line that connects points 1 and 3 cannot be horizontal; it has to slant at least slightly downwards. Similarly, in the trend line that connects 2–4 (the upper trend line) the degree of slant is always steeper than that of the trend line that connects points 1–3 (i.e. the lower trend line).

Case study - Nifty (Daily charts)

The Nifty was trending down from Apr 2011 to Dec 2012 before a bullish irregular diagonal developed. After the breakout from the pattern took place in Jan 2012 at 4900 levels the market hit the target level of 5600 within a month.

Nifty (daily)

Fig 7.3

Pattern: Bullish Irregular Diagonal

Entry point: The trend line connecting point 2 and 4 breaks at point 6 and signals an entry level for a buy trade at point 6, i.e. around 4850 levels.

Stop loss levels at entry: The stop loss is set at 4500 level (at point 5 in the above chart). This is the reaction low after point 4.

Exit Point: The extended trend line connecting point 1 and point 4 will be the exit level for the trade. In this case study, the exit level is marked as point 7 and happens around 5600.

Remember that point 1 to 5 in any irregular diagonal (bullish or bearish) will be pivots and point 5, being irregular, will always go below the trend line connecting point 1 and point 3 in a bullish irregular diagonal.

Bearish Irregular Diagonal

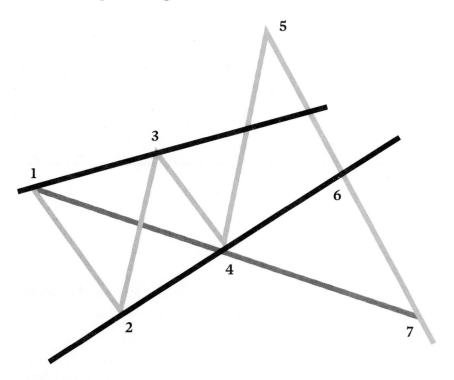

Fig 7.4

TECHNICAL ANALYSIS

RULES TO RECOGNIZE BEARISH IRREGULAR DIAGNALS:

In any irregular diagonal pattern, point 1 is always a pivot.

Point 2 is the reaction low of point 1

Point 3 is the reaction high of point 2 and point 3 is always higher than point 1

Point 4 is the reaction low of point 3 and point 4 is always higher than point 2

Point 5 is an irregular point that extends above the trend line that connects point 1 and point 3

Point 5 is also the stop loss point.

Point 6 is the sell point which is an extension of the trend line that connects point 2 and point 4.

Point 7 is the target point and is the extension of the trend line that connects point 1 and point 4.

In an irregular diagonal formation, the trend line formed by joining points 1-3 cannot be horizontal; it has to slant at least slightly up. It should also be noted that the slope of the trend line formed by joining points 2 and 4 (i.e. the lower trend line) is always steeper than that formed by joining points 1 and 3 (i.e. the lower trend line).

Case study – Nifty (Weekly Chart)

The Indian stock market had a dream run from 2003 and kept making consistently higher highs and lows, indicating an uptrend. However, this bull run came to an end in Jan 2008, in the form of an irregular diagonal. As seen in the Nifty chart, throughout the pattern, the prices kept making new highs on the weekly time frame but a sudden fall in prices caught the bulls off guard and they had to square up positions. Later, all fresh sell positions on the Nifty only aggravated the fall.

Nifty chart

Fig 7.5

Pattern: Bearish Irregular Diagonal

Entry point: The trend line connecting point 2 and 4 breaks at point 6 and we see an entry level in the form of a sell trade at point 6, around 5900 levels.

TECHNICAL ANALYSIS

Stop loss levels at entry: A stop loss is set at 6300 levels (at point 5 in the above chart). It should be noted that point 5 is the reaction high after point 4.

Exit Point: The extended trend line connecting points 1 and 4 will be the exit level for the trade. In this case study, the exit level is marked as point 7 and happens around 5400.

Points 1 to 5 in any irregular diagonal (bullish or bearish) will be pivots and point 5, being irregular, will always go above the trend line connecting point 1 and point 3, in case of a bearish irregular diagonal.

Case Studies of Bullish and Bearish Irregular Diagonals

Euro/USD chart (daily)

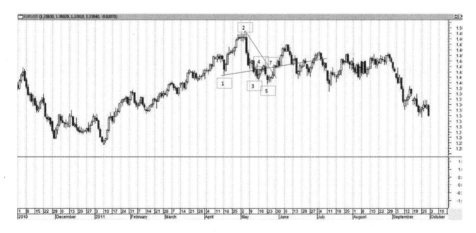

Fig 7.6

Pattern: Bullish Irregular Diagonal

Entry point: The trend line connecting point 2 and 4 breaks at point 6 and the entry level for a buy trade comes at point 6, around 1.41 levels.

Stop loss levels at entry: The stop loss is set at 1.39 (at point 5 in the above chart). This is the reaction low after point 4.

Exit Point: The extended trend line connecting point 1 and point 4 will be the exit level for the trade. In this case study the exit level is marked at point 7 and happened around 1.44.

In a bullish irregular diagonal, the trend line joining points 1 and 3 cannot be horizontal; it has to slant at least slightly down and further, the degree of slant of the trend line joining points 2 and 4 (i.e. the upper trend line) is always steeper than that of the trend line joining points 1 and 3 (lower trend line).

Crude price chart

Fig 7.7

Pattern: Bearish irregular diagonal

Entry point: The trend line connecting points 2 and 4 breaks at point 6 and the entry level for the sell trade comes at point 6 around USD 100 levels.

Stop loss levels at entry: The stop-loss is set at USD 110 (at point 5 in the above chart).

Exit Point: The extended trend line connecting point 1 and point 4 will be the exit level for the trade. In this case study, the exit level is marked as point 7 and the exit level is set around USD 85.

Crude has a great bull run from lows of USD 33 in Jan 2009 to a high of USD 114 in June 2011. However, in Apr 2012, the Bearish irregular diagonal pattern was complete, signaling a downturn in prices and after the entry trigger came, prices started to drop and the pattern hit a target inside 5 weeks after the break-out.

DJIA (weekly)

Fig 7.8

Pattern: Bullish irregular diagonal

Entry point: The trend line connecting point 2 and 4 breaks at point 6 and the entry level for the buy trade comes at point 6, around 10500 levels.

Stop loss levels at entry: The stop loss is set at 9500 (at point 5 in the above chart). It should be noted that point 5 is the reaction low after point 4.

Exit Point: The extended trend line connecting point 1 and point 4 will be the exit level for the trade. In this case study, the exit level is marked at point 7 and occurs at around 11500.

The bullish irregular diagonal observed in the Dow Jones chart marks a continuation in trend as a bullish trend was already in place from April 2009. Hence, we see that an irregular diagonal does not always change the trend. It can either contribute to a change in trend or act as a trigger for trend continuation.

Dell share price chart

Fig 7.9

Pattern: Bearish irregular diagonal

Entry point: The trend line connecting point 2 and 4 breaks at point 6 and the entry level for the sell trade comes at point 6 around 27 USD levels.

Stop loss levels at entry: The stop loss is set at USD 30 (at point 5 in the above chart).

Exit Point: The extended trend line connecting point 1 and point 4 will be the exit level for the trade. In this case study, the exit level is marked as point 7 and the exit level is set at around USD 23.

In most irregular diagonal formations, there is a high probability that the price will move in the same direction even after hitting the target. In this case study, we see how Dell's stock touches a low of USD 8 after hitting the target.

ITC share price chart

Fig 7.10

Pattern: Bullish irregular diagonal

Entry point: The trend line connecting point 2 and 4 breaks at point 6 and the entry level for a buy trade comes at point 6, at around Rs 90 levels.

Stop loss levels at entry: The stop loss is set at about Rs 70 (at point 5 in the above chart).

Exit Point: The extended trend line connecting point 1 and point 4 will be the exit level for the trade. In this case study, the exit level is marked as point 7 and the exit level is set around Rs 180.

The thought that FMCG stocks are stuck in a range was always questioned after this bullish irregular diagonal formed in ITC charts, taking the price of the stock to new all-time highs.

IDEA share price chart

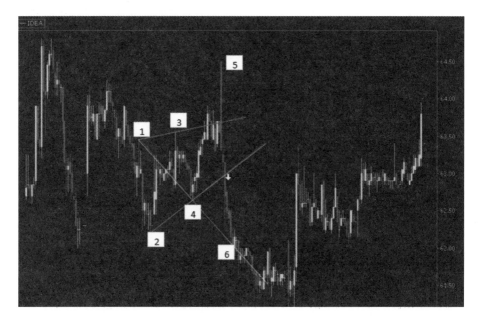

Fig 7.11

Pattern: Bearish irregular diagonal

Entry point: The trend line connecting point 2 and 4 breaks where we have the down arrow in the charts and the entry level for the sell trade comes around Rs 63.

Stop loss levels at entry: The stop loss is set at Rs 64.5 (at point 5 in the above chart).

Exit Point: The extended trend line connecting point 1 and point 4 will be the exit level for the trade. In this case study, the exit level is marked as point 6 and the exit level is set around Rs 62.

Irregular diagonal formations are not confined to timeframes like Monthly, Weekly and Daily alone; they can occur in any timeframe, just like other patterns discussed in earlier chapters.

RCom share price chart

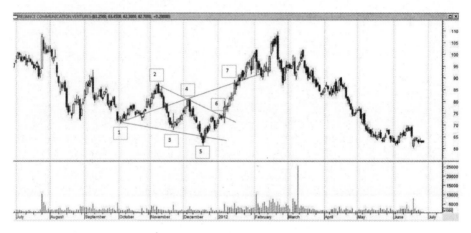

Fig 7.12

Pattern: Bullish irregular diagonal

Entry point: The trend line connecting point 2 and 4 breaks at point 6 and the entry level for a buy trade comes at point 6 around Rs 72 levels.

Stop loss levels at entry: The stop loss is set at about Rs 60. (at point 5 in the above chart).

Exit Point: The extended trend line connecting point 1 and point 4 will be the exit level for the trade. In this case study, the exit level is marked as point 7 and the exit level is set around Rs 90.

In spite of the stock following a downtrend when this pattern occurred, the target was achieved within 8 days after the break-out happened. So it is important to keep the natural bias away while trading (if it is a buy signal we buy at the entry trigger level and don't think about whether the stock is following a downtrend or a sideways trend) .

Gold price chart (daily)

Fig 7.13

Pattern: Bearish irregular diagonal

Entry point: The trend line connecting points 2 and 4 breaks at point 6 in the charts and the entry level for a sell trade comes around

12,700 levels.

Stop loss levels at entry: Stop loss is set at around 14,200 (at point 5 in the above chart).

Exit point: The extended trend line connecting point 1 and point 4 will be the exit level for the trade. In this case study the exit level is marked as point 7 and the exit level is set around 11,300 levels.

As mentioned earlier, all the points, from point 1 to point 5, will always be pivots in an irregular diagonal pattern and it is extremely important to have a good understanding of pivots before trading irregular diagonals.

Closing Note:

The five most important set-ups have been covered from Chapters 3 to 7 and by now it will be very clear that without an in-depth understanding of Pivots, it will be very difficult to trade patterns like Double tops/bottoms, Head and Shoulders and Irregular Diagonals. Hence, it is important that you are thorough with Chapter 3 and can identify pivots very clearly, before moving any further. To become very thorough with Pivots, you could take price charts (at least 100 across timeframes and asset classes) and start marking pivots and check whether all the rules that you have understood in Chapter 3 have been followed, before venturing in to actual trading. Beginners and even experienced technicians will find that identifying irregular diagonals is the most difficult, especially in intra-day timeframes, from among all set-ups discussed in this book. So practice hard before putting your money into real-time trading/investing.

Exercises

Irregular Diagonals

1) ***Irregular Diagonals closely resemble which two popular patterns?***

A) Head & Shoulders

B) Tops and Bottoms

C) Wedges

Answer: $\boxed{\text{C}}$

---

2) ***Name the irregular point(s) in the Irregular Diagonals pattern?***

A) Point 5 and Point 3

B) Point 3

C) Point 5

Answer: $\boxed{\text{B}}$

3) *Mark the Irregular Diagonal patterns in the Maruti Weekly charts below, if any*

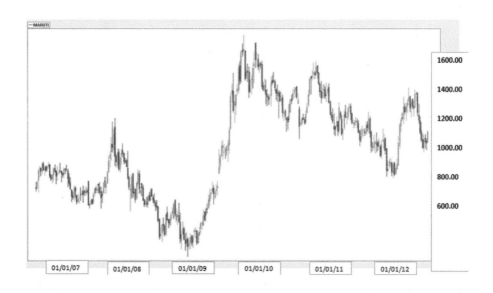

Answer:

There were three bullish Irregular Diagonals on the charts. While the first and third Bullish Irregular Diagonal hit the target, the second one triggered a stop-loss. Point 7 is the exit point in the below chart and the second bullish irregular diagonal after giving entry at point 6 went below the stop-loss level (point 5) at point 7, while the first and third patterns had their exit points at the target level (point 7).

4) Mark the Irregular Diagonal patterns in the Master Card Daily charts below, if any

Answer:

There were two Irregular Diagonals on the chart. While the first one was bearish, the second one was bullish and both hit their respective target points (marked as 7 in the chart).

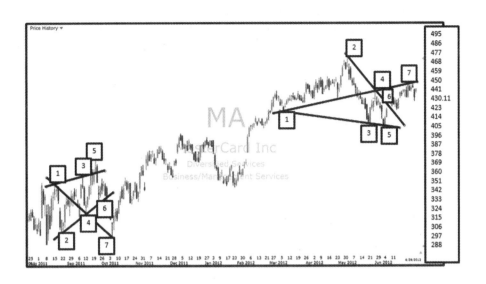

TEST PERFORMANCE OF DOUBLE TOPS AND BOTTOMS, HEAD AND SHOULDERS AND IRREGULAR DIAGONALS ON PAST DATA OF NIFTY

(weekly and daily timeframes) →

CHAPTER 8

*U*nderstanding the rules and trade setups for three main patterns – Double tops/bottoms (DT/DB), Head and Shoulders (HS) and Irregular Diagonals (ID) - is extremely important in technical analysis based trading, as these are the most reliable and important patterns. In just 13 trades on the Nifty between 2008 and 2010, these 3 patterns alone have delivered 5,216 points. This is precisely the reason why these patterns have been given a lot of emphasis in this book. They usually work across timeframes, asset classes and geographies.

Nifty Trades Data (2008-2010)

S.NO	DATE	PATTERN	TARGET pts/duration per lot	PROFIT/LOSS
1	18-01-2008	ID bearish weekly	550/1WEEK	550
2	03-03-2008	DT daily	314/4 days	314
3	06-06-2008	HS bearish weekly	1700/20weeks	1700
4	15-09-2008	HS bearish daily	400/4 weeks	400
5	17-02-2009	ID bearish daily	270/12 days	270
6	02-04-2009	HS bullish daily	600/43days	600
7	02-04-2009	DB weekly	600/43days	600
8	16-06-2009	ID bearish daily	200/2 days	200
9	06-08-2009	ID bearish daily	300/5days	300
10	31-07-2009	HS bullish daily	-218	-218
11	24-08-2009	DB daily	270/23days	270
12	15-12-2009	DT daily	-140	-140
13	21-01-2010	ID bearish daily	370/5 days	370
			Total	**5216**

Fig 8.1

DT = *double top,* **DB** = *Double bottom,* **HS** = *head and shoulders,* **ID** = *Irregular diagonal*

Case Study from Back-test sheet: Bearish Irregular Diagonal – NIFTY FUTURES (DAILY)

The irregular diagonal in the Nifty futures daily chart below forms the basis for the 13th entry in the back test sheet above. As mentioned earlier, irregular diagonals take lesser time to achieve their targets than most other technical analysis patterns. In the chart below, the bearish irregular diagonal gave 370 points in just 5 trading days.

Bearish Irregular Diagonal

Fig 8.2

As an exercise, spot the other 12 patterns, as mentioned in the back test sheet, and mark the entry, exit and stop loss levels.

OTHER PATTERNS OF SIGNIFICANCE

CHAPTER 9

V and Inverted V - Spikes

Overview

C ontrary to most patterns which warn us about imminent changes in trend, a spike suddenly reverses the trend with little warning. Apart from spikes all patterns offer trading opportunities; with spikes it is difficult to trade as the pattern itself is complete once a significant and swift move takes place. A 'V' reverses the trend from down to up while an inverted V reverses the trend from up to down.

As the name suggests, a V spike looks like the letter v, while an inverted V spike looks like the letter V flipped upside down.

Case Study: DJIA (Weekly)

The chart below shows a V spike on the Dow Jones weekly charts. In fact, this spike took the Dow Jones from 6500 to nearly 9000.

DJIA chart (weekly)

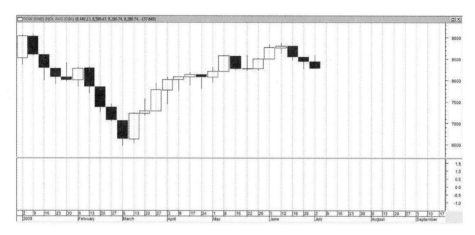

Fig 9.1

Case Study: ADLABS (Weekly)

An inverted V pattern leads to a price crash in Adlabs Weekly timeframe charts from Rs 1800 to under Rs 200 levels

Adlabs price chare (weekly)

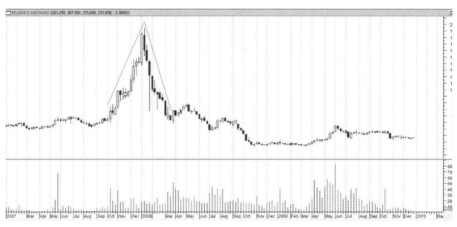

Fig 9.2

Both V and inverted V spikes are commonly found in illiquid stock (stocks where the trading volumes are low) as a small amount of buying or selling is enough to push the price up or down. Hence, from a risk perspective, it's important for traders and investors to avoid stocks which have very small trading volume.

As mentioned earlier, V and inverted V spikes cannot be traded and though it's important to know the pattern, it has been included in this book for information only.

TRIANGLES

Overview

There are different types of triangles that frequent price charts. All these triangles show a compression in demand and supply throughout the pattern before price eventually breaks. The four main types of triangles are:-

→ Symmetrical triangle

→ Ascending triangle

→ Descending triangle

→ Wedge

Symmetrical Triangle

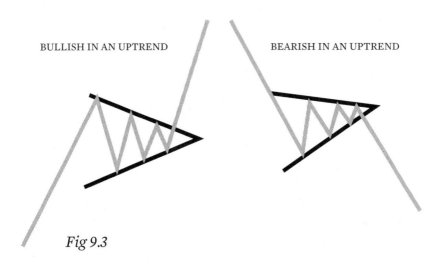

BULLISH IN AN UPTREND   BEARISH IN AN UPTREND

Fig 9.3

TECHNICAL ANALYSIS

Symmetrical triangles can be characterized as areas of indecision. In such patterns, the market pauses and the future direction is questioned. Typically, the forces of supply and demand at that moment are considered nearly equal. Attempts to push higher are quickly met by selling, while dips are seen as bargains. Each new lower top and higher bottom becomes more shallow than the last, taking on the shape of a sideways triangle. Interestingly, there is a tendency for volume to diminish during this period. Eventually, this indecision is met with resolve and usually explodes out of this formation, often with heavy volumes. Research has shown that symmetrical triangles overwhelmingly resolve themselves in the direction of the trend. With this in mind, symmetrical triangles are great patterns to use and should be traded as continuation patterns.

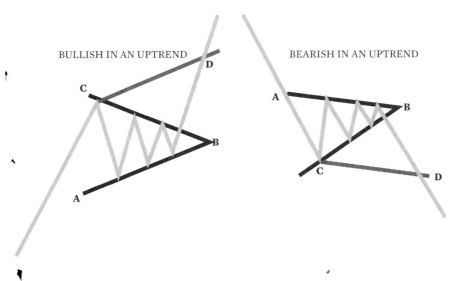

SYMMETRIC TRIANGLE

BULLISH IN AN UPTREND

BEARISH IN AN UPTREND

As we can see from the above image, the target for symmetric triangle is the line that connects CD and this runs parallel to the line that connects AB. The buy signal gets generated when prices breach line CB on the upside in a bullish symmetric triangle pattern and the sell signal gets generated when prices breach line CB on the downside in a bearish symmetric triangle pattern.

Hexaware price chart (daily)

Fig 9.4

Pattern: Symmetric Triangle – Bullish

Entry point: The entry comes with a buy trade when trend line CB breaks on the upside at Rs 40 approximately, as denoted by the up arrow in the charts.

Stop loss levels at entry: Point A, which is around Rs 20 in the chart, will be the stop loss level.

Exit Point: Rs 60, i.e.point D, will be the exit level;

TECHNICAL ANALYSIS

You will notice that the trend-line CD (target trend-line) always runs parallel to trend line AB.

Gold chart (daily)

Fig 9.5

Pattern: Symmetric Triangle – Bearish

Entry point: The entry comes with a sell trade when trend line CB breaks on the downside at 27300, as denoted by a down arrow in the chart.

Stop loss levels at entry: Point A which is at around 28,800 in the chart will be the stop loss level.

Exit Point: Point D, i.e. 26,300 will be the exit level

You will notice that the trend-line CD (target trend-line) always runs parallel to trend line AB.

Though symmetric triangles resolve themselves in the direction of the trend, in the above chart the trend was up before the bearish pattern occurred. Hence the underlying trend could only provide us with a hint. However, the decision to buy or sell is based purely on the pattern trigger only.

ASCENDING TRIANGLE AND DESCENDING TRIANGLE

Overview

Ascending and descending triangles

ASCENDING TRIANGLE - BULLISH

DESCENDING TRIANGLE - BEARISH

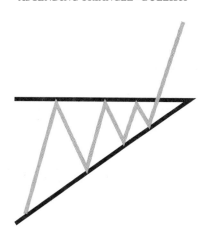
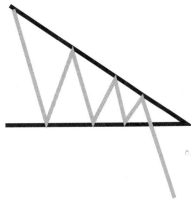

Fig 9.6

Ascending triangle: In ascending triangle, throughout the pattern, the price continues to make higher bottoms (represented in Fig 9.6

by an upward sloping trendline), while facing steady resistance at a certain level (the horizontal top trendline in the above image). When prices making higher bottoms, it means that demand is growing and once all the supply at the resistance level is absorbed, prices will breakout and move up at a rapid rate.

Descending triangle: This pattern is the opposite of an ascending triangle. Here, the supply keeps growing, but demand comes in at a certain level. Eventually, when the demand is exhausted, prices breakout and move lower at a rapid pace.

Ascending (Bullish) and descending (Bearish) triangles

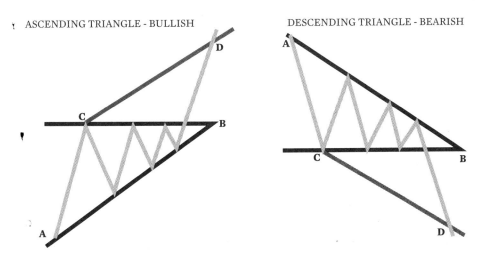

Fig 9.7

As we can see from Fig.9.7, the target for ascending and descending triangles is the line that joins points C and D and this line runs parallel to AB. The buy signal gets generated when prices breach line CB on the upside in an ascending triangle pattern and the sell signal gets generated when prices breach line CB on the downside in a descending triangle pattern.

Morgan Stanley price chart (monthly)

Fig 9.8

Pattern: Ascending Triangle

Entry point: The buy entry is triggered when the resistance for prices to move up breaks at USD 54 (denoted by the up arrow in the charts).

Stop loss levels at entry: The price level of USD 24 is the lowest pivotal point of the pattern (represented by point A in the above chart).

TECHNICAL ANALYSIS

Exit Point: USD 75 (i.e. Point D) will be the exit level and the trend-line CD (target trend-line) always runs parallel to trend line AB.

ICICI Bank ADS (daily)

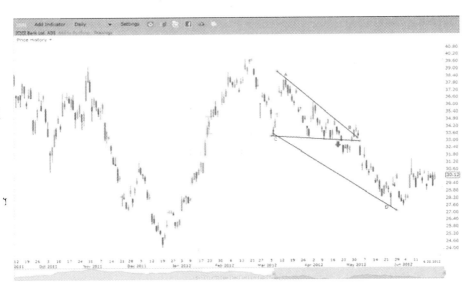

Fig 9.9

Pattern: Descending Triangle

Entry point: The sell side entry occurs at USD 33 when the support level is broken on the downside (marked with down arrow in the charts).

Stop loss levels at entry: Point A as shown in the charts will be the stop loss area (around 39 USD) and Point A also happens to be the highest point the pattern.

Exit Point: The trend line parallel to AB acts as the target area. In this case study the target is marked at D around the USD 27 level.

Ascending, descending and symmetric triangles are rarely found in long-term timeframes and can be found in short-term charts like daily and intra-day timeframes. However, they are not significant patterns and are prone to false break-outs (a break-out which immediately reverses after entry in to the trade and hits stop-loss levels) and hence, should be traded with caution.

WEDGES

Overview

Wedges

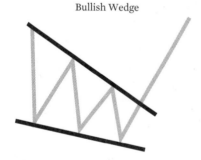
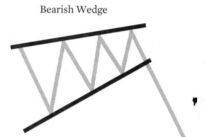

Fig 9.10

Wedges are formed when prices fluctuate between two converging trend-lines. For a bullish wedge (falling wedge) the lines are slanted downwards and the upper line is steeper than the lower line. For a bearish wedge (rising wedge) the lines are slanted upwards and the lower line is steeper than the upper line. Further, bullish wedge represents a scenario where, even though the prices are making lower tops, the supply is slowly diminishing and vice-versa for a bearish wedge. Once prices break through the upper trend-line in a bullish wedge, a buy signal is generated and as the lower trend-line breaks, a sell signal is generated in case of bearish wedge. Wedges look similar to Irregular Diagonals except for the irregular fifth wave but wedges can also make more than 5 waves inside the pattern before breaking out in either direction. Another key point to note is that Wedges don't have a specific target area. Due to this feature, i.e. not having a target, we use pivot breaks as exits.

Nifty chart (weekly)

Fig 9.11

Pattern: Bullish Wedge

Entry point: The entry on the pattern was at 900 levels in Jan 1999 when the resistance trend-line was broken on the Upside (marked with up arrow in the charts).

Stop loss levels at entry: For any bullish wedge, the lowest point in the pattern will be the stop loss area (around 800 levels in the chart).

Exit Point: The first pivot break after the entry area will act as the exit point (the pivot break must take place opposite to the direction of the trade entered, i.e., in this case study, the entry was on the buy side, hence we wait till the pivot triggers a downtrend to exit from the sell trade). In this case study, the first pivot break happened around 1300 levels in Nov 1999.

Morgan Stanley price chart (daily)

Fig 9.12

Pattern: Bearish Wedge

Entry point: The sell entry on the pattern happened at 18.5 USD levels in Apr 2012 when the support trend-line was broken on the downside (marked with a down arrow in the charts).

Stop loss levels at entry: For any bearish wedge, the highest point in the pattern will be the stop loss area (around USD 21.5 levels in the chart).

Exit Point: The first pivot break after the entry area will act as the exit point (the pivot break must happen opposite to the direction of the trade entered, i.e. in this case study, the entry was on the sell side, hence we wait till a pivot triggers an uptrend to exit from the sell trade). In this case study, the first pivot break occurs around 13.50 levels in June 2012.

FLAGS

Overview

Flags

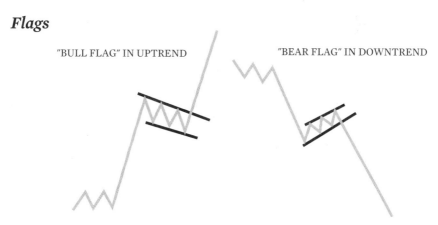

"BULL FLAG" IN UPTREND   "BEAR FLAG" IN DOWNTREND

Fig 9.13

FLAGS

In a flag pattern, prices move sideways, forming a flag-like pattern. They then break out from that pattern, and then continue in the same direction as before.

Bullish flags are characterized by lower tops and lower bottoms, with the pattern slanting against the trend. Their trend-lines run parallel.

Bearish flags are comprised of higher tops and higher bottoms. "Bear" flags also have a tendency to slope against the trend. Their trend-lines run parallel as well.

Flags are not usually traded as they do not have specific areas that can be delineated for exit from a trade. Flags only tell us whether a uptrend or downtrend is likely to continue and they are usually found when a strong trending move (either up or down) is in place in long-term charts (weekly, monthly and quarterly).

Nifty chart (weekly)

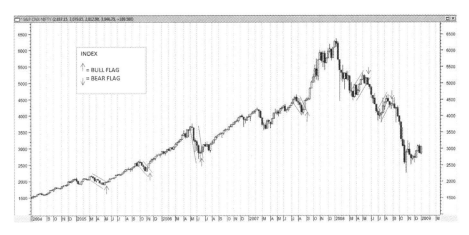

Fig 9.14

In the above Nifty weekly charts, we can see multiple bullish flags during the period when the strong uptrend was in place, between July 2004 and Jan 2008. However, after Jan 2008, when the downtrend started (and continued till early 2009), bearish flags can be spotted at frequent intervals on the charts.

Flags have been included in this book for academic interest only and investors/traders should avoid trading them.

TREND CHANNELS

Overview

Trend channels occur when prices move within a range in between two trend-lines. The trend-lines in a trend channel are mostly parallel and may have a bias either towards an upside or downside.

The trend channel with an upside bias is called an uptrend channel and the trend channel with a downside bias is called a downtrend channel. When the trend-lines don't have a bias (either up or down), we refer to such a scenario as a side-ways channel (the market terminology used is range-bound when prices keep fluctuating between approximately similar resistance and support levels).

In a downtrend channel, we keep selling as the price hits the upper end of the trend channel and exit when the price hits the lower end and vice-versa in case of an uptrend channel. This is done to ensure that our trades are in the direction of the trend and, in fact, following the trend.

In a side-ways trend channel, we buy at the lower end of the band and place stop and reverse trades at the upper end (i.e. if we bought x quantity during entry, we sell 2x quantity during the following exit, as each buy position is followed by a sell position and so on and so forth).

CASE STUDIES FOR TREND CHANNELS

GBP/USD chart (weekly)

Fig 9.15

Pattern: Uptrend Channel

Entry point: The buy entry came at 1.96 levels in late Aug 2007 when the support trend-line (AB in the above charts) was tested for the third time. As mentioned in chapter 1, the higher the number of times a trend-line is tested, the more the importance increases (the buy area is marked with an up arrow in the charts).

Stop loss levels at entry: The stop-loss will be 2% below the entry point (in case of a downtrend channel we take a stop loss at 2% above the entry point).

Exit Point: The exit area will be the upper end of the channel (CD in the above case study) and the exit came in at 2.10 levels in Nov 2007.

The upper end of any trend channel is called the resistance and the low end is called support. In this case study, it is curious to note how the prices started collapsing after the support trend line AB was broken. Hence we usually avoid entering when the same support level is tested again and again as the probability of hitting our stop-loss increases with each successive price re-test.

Nifty chart (weekly)

Fig 9.16

Pattern: Downtrend Channel

Entry point: The sell entry came at 5400 levels in Oct 2011 when the resistance trend-line (AB in the above charts) was tested for the fifth time. As mentioned in chapter 1, the more often a trend-line is tested the greater its importance becomes (the sell area is marked with a down arrow in the charts).

Stop loss levels at entry: The stop-loss will be 2% above the entry point (in case of an uptrend channel we take a stop loss at 2% below the entry point).

Exit Point: The exit area will be the upper end of the channel (CD in the above case study) and the exit came in at 4600 levels in Dec 2011.

CBOE VIX chart (monthly)

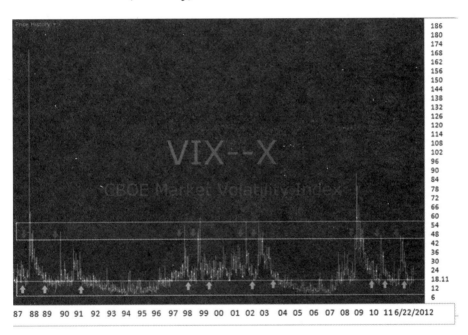

Fig 9.17

Pattern: Sideways Channel

Entry point: The entry point for a trade entered on a sideways channel will be the support point. A relatively safe strategy would be to buy VIX at 19 levels and hold it, as periods of low volatility will be followed by periods of high volatility.

Stop loss levels at entry: The stop-loss point for such trades usually will be 2% below the support point. In the above case study the stop-loss point will be 8 (which incidentally is the all-time low VIX made in 2007).

Exit Point: The exit area will be the resistance level, in this case study it's 46.

The above chart shows that the CBOE – Volatility Index, which measures market risk (VIX readings are high when the market witnesses sharp volatility usually on the downside) has been within a channel since 1987, except for a few periods where it broke through the resistance as well. There have only been three instances since 1987, when VIX readings started, where the upper resistance band of 46 – 58 has been broken and in all three instances. This occurred in the month of October, which also shows that the month of October can be extremely volatile.

Most volatile days in VIX's recorded history: In 1987, VIX made a high of 172 when Dow Jones crashed 22.61% in a single day on 19th of October 1987 which is the largest single day percentage drop in Dow Jones' History. Later in 1998, VIX made a high of 60 when Dow Jones lost about 7% on 27th of October 1998 during the Dot-com bubble and in Oct 2008 VIX made a high of 89 during the heydays of global financial crisis when Dow Jones lost more than 7% each on 9th and 15th of October. Even before 1987, October has seen many single day crashes and a case in point would be the 1929 crash which started the great depression when Dow Jones fell more than 10% each on 28th and 29th of October. Since 1896, when Dow Jones Industrial Average was found by Dow, there have been 19 instances where Dow Jones has lost more than 7% in a single day and out of the 19, 9 happened in October.

Closing Note: Trend channels are prone to false break-outs hence it may not be a prudent idea to trade them unless it's a side-ways trend channel, which may work in specific asset classes (like CBOE-VIX).

Candlestick patterns

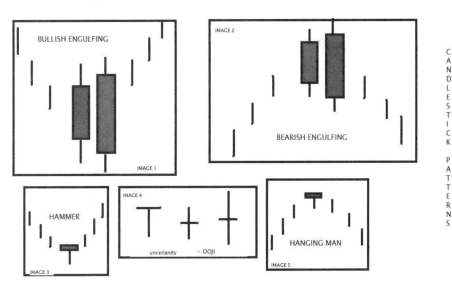

Fig 9.18

BULLISH ENGULFING (IMAGE 1)

A bullish engulfing occurs when prices open lower than the previous period's close and then rally to close above the previous period's open. Thus the current period's green body engulfs the previous period's red body. Per say, shadows are ignored in this pattern. This pattern signals a reversal of trend from bearish to bullish.

BEARISH ENGULFING (IMAGE 2)

Bearish engulfing is the opposite of bullish engulfing. The main difference is that bearish engulfing takes place after an uptrend in prices and signals a reversal of trend from up to down. In this pattern, the previous period's green body is engulfed by the current period's red body. In this pattern too, shadows are ignored. This pattern signals a reversal of trend from bullish to bearish

All the up arrows in the Nifty intra-day options chart below are bullish engulfing while the down arrows are bearish engulfing.

Nifty chart (intra day)

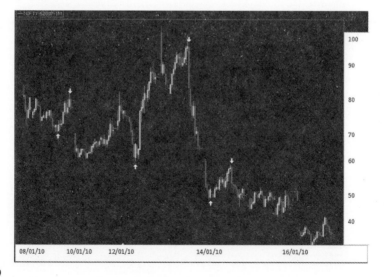

Fig 9.19

TECHNICAL ANALYSIS

HAMMER (IMAGE 3):

A hammer occurs when prices rally from an intra-period sell off to close near the open. This results in the main body, which can be either green or red being at the higher end of the period with little or no upper shadow. The lower shadow must be at least twice the length of the main body to be considered a genuine hammer.

A hammer pattern should be traded as a bullish reversal signal only when the market is in a down move. The hammer gets its name from the fact that it usually hammers out the bottom.

DOJI (IMAGE 4)

This pattern occurs when the period's opening price and the closing price are the same and indicates uncertainty in both the bull and bear camp.

HANGING MAN (IMAGE 5)

The Hanging man pattern is the opposite of the Hammer, as the hammer takes place after a downtrend and the hanging man occurs after an uptrend. The hanging man also signals a reversal in trend.

Closing Note: Though very popular among technicians, none of the candle stick patterns contribute significantly to a trader's or investor's bottom line as they don't have any measuring implications. Further, they usually do not convey whether a trend has changed. Hence candle patterns have been included for academic interest only.

Exercises

Other Patterns of Significance

1) Diagonals V and Inverted V – Spike patterns can be traded

A) Yes, they are great patterns to trade

B) No, they cannot be traded and they don't provide any warning about a imminent change in trend

C) No, as they are difficult patterns to trade and don't appear very frequently on the charts

Answer: B

2) Can you spot any triangle patterns in the EUR/USD chart below?

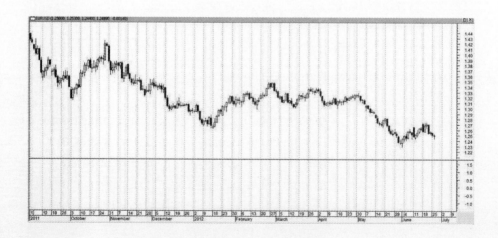

Answer:	Yes there was a descending triangle visible on the charts which pushed the EURO to a new low not seen since July 2010 against the USD.

3)   *In the GBP/USD weekly charts below, how many triangle patterns can you spot?*

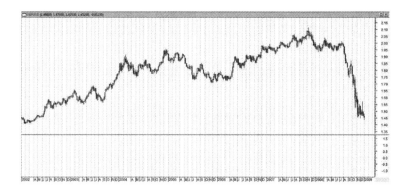

Also check how the trend-line AB is parallel to the target trend-line CD

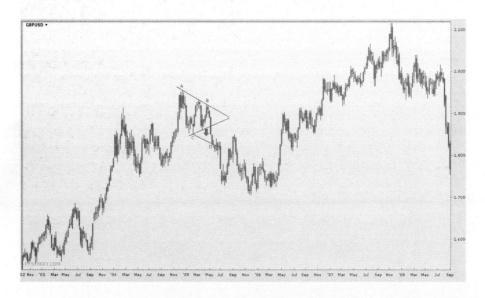

4) *Mark all the bullish and bearish engulfing candle stick patterns which lead to a turnaround in prices in the Standard and Poor's 500 (SPX) chart below.*

Answer: 'A bearish engulfing pattern can be seen inside all oval boxes while bullish engulfing pattern can be found inside the square boxes.

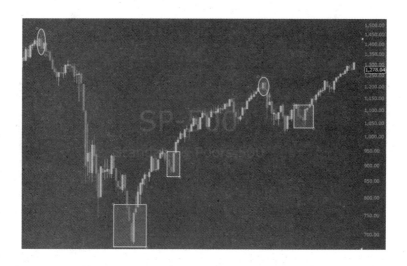

TOOLS TO SUPPLEMENT YOUR TRADES

CHAPTER 10

INDICATORS

*T*he market can move in three directions - upwards, downwards or sideways. Both upward and downward movements in markets are classified as trending moves and the price movements in which the market is stuck in a range or without any directional bias are called trading moves.

In a trending market we follow indicators like Moving Average Convergence and Divergence (MACD), moving averages and so on.

In a trading market we use indicators such as oscillators like Relative Strength Index (RSI), stochastics, etc.

What is ADX

ADX or Average Directional Movement is an indicator which depicts the underlying strength of the trend. It is non-directional so it will quantify a trend's strength regardless of whether it is upwards or downwards. ADX is usually plotted in a chart with two lines known as the DMI (Directional Movement Indicators). ADX is derived from the relationship of the DMI lines. Analysis of ADX helps traders to choose the strongest trends and ensure the profits are not taken out as long as the trend is strong.

What is DM?

Directional Movement (DM) is the difference between the high and low of a period that falls outside the range of the previous period. Irrespective of the timeframe used, price movements above the previous periods high are positive directional movements (+ DM) and those below the previous period low are negative directional movement (- DM).

DMI

A Directional Indicator (DI) is found by dividing the positive DM and negative DM over a 14 bar period. Long trades are entered into when +DI moves over –DI and vice-versa, for short trades. DMI should be applied on volatile asset classes and works well on the USD/JPY currency pair and interest rate sensitive stocks.

Case study : USD / JPY (weekly)

In the USD/JPY weekly chart we just buy when the positive DM crosses the negative DM from below and vice versa for sell trades. In the chart below, up arrows depict buy areas and down arrows depict sell areas. Since the trend is predominantly down in the chart below, we will only enter sell trades and exit when the buy trigger comes. Remember we should always go with the flow of the market and not against it.

USD/JPY chart (weekly)

Fig 10.1

Case study: SBI (weekly)

In the SBI weekly chart below, we just buy when the green line (the positive DM) crosses the red line (the negative DM) from below and vice-versa for sell trades. The up arrow shows the buy areas and down arrows show the sell areas. Since there is a strong trend in both directions, we follow the stop and reverse rule.

SBI price chart (weekly)

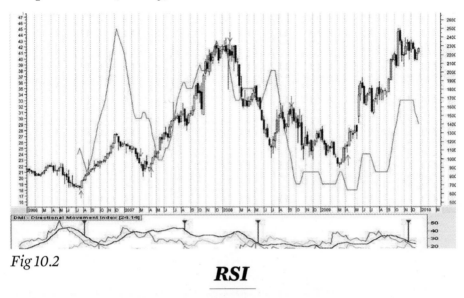

Fig 10.2

RSI

What Does Relative Strength Index- RSI Mean?

RSI is a momentum indicator that compares the magnitude of recent gains to recent losses in an attempt to determine overbought and oversold conditions of an asset. It is calculated using the following formula:

$$\textbf{RSI} = 100 - \frac{100}{1 + RS}$$

RS = Average of x days' up closes / Average of x days' down closes

The RSI ranges from 0 to 100. An asset is deemed to be overbought once the RSI approaches the 70 level, meaning that it may be getting overvalued and is a good candidate for a pullback. Likewise, if the RSI approaches 30, it is an indication that the asset may be getting oversold and is, therefore, likely to become undervalued.

We use oscillators such as the RSI (which is a lead oscillator), when stocks are stuck in a trading range for a long time, as is often the case with defensive stocks like Pharma and FMCG sector stocks.

Case study: Coke

We take the following Coke chart as a case study to better understand RSI. The buy and sell signals in the chart below are custom made and not the usual buy at 30 and sell at 70.

The support RSI is taken around 42 for this stock because it is the level from where the RSI has bounced back to touch the resistance band of 62 previously. The higher the number of times a support RSI is touched the higher its significance. The same logic applies to resistance RSI also. We buy when the stock hits the support RSI and sell when it hits the resistance RSI.

Coke price chart

Fig 10.3

In the above chart, the first entry came around USD 32 levels and exit at USD 58 level while the second entry came at USD 48 levels and the exit at USD 68.

The key point to be noted here is that RSI works well only on those asset classes which are stuck in a range for a long time hence should not be used with asset classes that keeps giving breakouts on either side (up or down). Even in those range bound stocks we should find the support and resistance RSI ourselves and then start trading them rather than the standard settings in most technical analysis software which gives a buy signal at 30 and sell signal at 70.

RSI

What Does Moving Average Convergence Divergence (MACD) Mean?

MACD is a trend-following momentum indicator that shows the relationship between two moving averages of prices. The MACD is calculated by subtracting the 26-day exponential moving average (EMA) from the 12-day EMA. A nine-day EMA of the MACD, called the "signal line", is then plotted on top of the MACD, functioning as a trigger for buy and sell signals. For trending markets we use MACD, moving averages and so on. So the application of MACD is confined to asset classes that trend, for example, interest rate sensitive stocks from sectors like banking, brokerage and real estate.

Case Study: UNITECH

In the chart below, we see the effectiveness of MACD signals on UNITECH weekly charts. All buy areas are plotted in the chart with up arrows and all sell areas are plotted with down arrows.

UNITECH price chart (weekly)

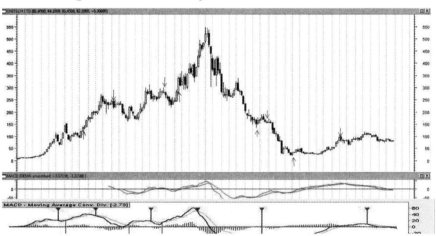

Fig 10.4

Bollinger Band

This term refers to a band plotted two standard deviations away from a simple moving average, developed by famous technical trader John Bollinger.

Because standard deviation is a measure of volatility, Bollinger bands adjust themselves to the market conditions. When the markets become more volatile, the bands widen (i.e. they move further away from the average) and during less volatile periods, the bands contract (i.e. they move closer to the average). The tightening of the bands is often used by technical traders as an early indication that the volatility is about to increase sharply.

This is one of the most popular technical analysis techniques. The closer the prices move to the upper band, the more overbought the market is and the closer the prices move to the lower band, the more oversold the market is.

Case study: Citibank charts

As noticed from the CITIBANK chart, the band got narrow between Jan 05 to Nov 08 and this was followed by prices moving down at a rapid pace. The take away from Bollinger bands is that when the price of an asset moves outside the band, it will revisit the area inside the band, providing some trading opportunities. However, it's not a great idea to build a system around this alone.

Citibank price chart

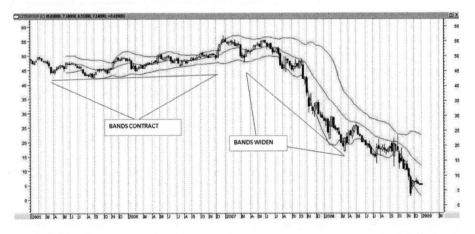

Fig 10.5

FIBONACCI SERIES

Leonard Fibonacci, a famous Italian mathematician, discovered the Fibonacci series.

The ratios arise from the following number series: 1, 1, 2, 3, 5, 8, 13, 21, 34, 55, 89, 144 ......This series of numbers is derived by starting with 1 followed by another 1 and then adding 1 + 1 to get 2, the third number. Then, adding 2 + 3 to get 5, the fourth number in the series, and so on.

After the first few numbers in the sequence, if you measure the ratio of any number to the subsequent one in the series, you get .618. For example, 34 divided by 55 equals 0.618.

For trading the key ratios are:

Fibonacci Retracement Levels: Fibonacci replacement levels comprise five ratios, namely 0.236, 0.382, 0.500, 0.618 and 0.764. To illustrate their use, if a stock is at 100 and the stock rose from zero, we expect the stock to gain support at 76.4, 61.8, 50. 38 or 23.6.Within these retracement levels, .382, .50 and .618 are the most important ones.

Fibonacci Extension Levels: These comprise 0, 0.382, 0.618, 1.000, 1.382, 1.618, 2.618, 4.236. To illustrate their use, if a stock moves beyond 100 from zero then we expect the stock to find resistance at 138.2, 161.8, 261.8 or 423.6. Within these 1.618, 2.618 and 4.236 are the key levels.

Any retracement or extension level is found by applying these Fibonacci sequence levels to swing highs and lows, depending upon whether we want to buy or sell. Fibonacci (Fib) ratios work reasonably well on long term charts only. Application of these ratios on intra-day chart should be avoided.

Hang Seng Index chart

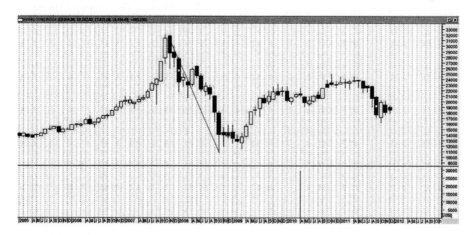

Fig 10.6

In the above monthly chart of the Hang Seng Index, we plot the fib retracement ratios from point A to Point B. Both the points are the respective reaction high (formed in Nov 2007) and reaction low (formed in Oct 2008). We mark the retracement levels to gauge the resistance area. From the above chart we could see that the Index had resistance at 61.8 retracement levels and has failed to cross that level as on July 2012.

S&P chart

Fig 10.7

In the above monthly chart of SPX, we plot the fib extension ratios from point A to Point B. Both the points are the respective reaction low (formed in Oct 2002) and reaction high (formed in Dec 2002). We mark the extension level to know where the uptrend could potentially end. From the above chart we can see that the uptrend move ended exactly at the fib extension level of 423.6, when SPX was trading around 1550 in Oct 2007. Fib extension levels could help when we have already entered the stock but don't know when to exit.

Trading Indicator Divergence

Divergence is a scenario where the price and indicators move in opposite directions. There are potentially two scenarios wherein divergence occurs.

1. Prices move up but indicators go down, thereby failing to match up with the bullishness in price. This is called negative divergence.

2. Price moves down but indicators go up, thereby indicating a turnaround in prices. This is called positive divergence.

The DJIA quarterly log chart below illustrates negative divergence between price and RSI. While RSI was going down, the price made fresh highs on the Dow Jones. This negative divergence was found in 2007 and lead to a massive price correction in the DJIA in 2008.

DJIA log chart (quarterly)

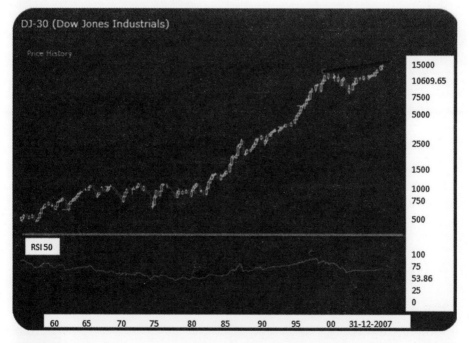

Fig 10.8

TECHNICAL ANALYSIS

OPEN INTEREST

Open interest refers to the number of outstanding derivative contracts in the market. In other words, open interest refers to the total number of derivative contracts that have not yet been liquidated by either an offsetting trade or an exercise or assignment. In essence, it is the sum of open positions waiting to be liquidated before the contract's expiry.

HOW IS IT COMPUTED?

Example of open interest computation

DATE	TRANSACTION	OPEN INTEREST
OCT 1	'A' buys 10 options and 'B' sells 10 options contracts	10
OCT 2	'C' buys 20 options and 'D' sells 20 options contracts	30
OCT 3	'A' Sells 10 options and 'D' buys 10 options contracts	20
OCT 4	'E' buys 20 options and 'C' sells 20 options contracts	20

Fig 10.9

On Oct 1, A buys 10 options and B sells them, creating an open interest of 10.

On Oct 2, C buys 20 options from D, thereby taking the open positions to 30.

On Oct 3, A squares–up his open position and reduces the open interest by 10.

On Oct 4, C also offsets his buy position, thereby leaving open interest unchanged.

From the above illustration, it is clear that we need to take into account the open positions on one side of the market only, either the longs or the shorts.

DIFFERENCE BETWEEN VOLUME AND OI

A common misconception is that open interest is the same thing as volume of derivative trades. This is not correct as Volume is the total number of contracts traded. So, for example, 10 contracts may have changed hands today, thereby creating a trading volume of 10 but still the open interest may be unchanged. This is because all transactions may have been squared-up, thereby leaving no open positions. In the above illustration, the volume of all transactions will be 80 while the open interest is only 20.

OPEN INTEREST AND VOLUME – IMPLICATIONS

Open interest (OI) is an indicator which tells us the direction of money flows in to and out of derivatives, which in turn affects the underlying stocks. OI can also give us an insight into the strength of the current trend. If OI is increasing in the direction of the trend (either upwards or downwards), then the probability of prices continuing their current trend increases. On the other hand, a decline in OI alerts us to an impending reversal or consolidation. It should be noted here that both OI and volume have similar implication as shown in the table:

Open interest and volume

PRICE	OPEN INTEREST/ VOLUME	IMPLICATION
RISING	UP	BULLISH
FALLING	UP	BEARISH
RISING	DOWN	BEARISH
FALLING	DOWN	BULLISH

Fig 10.10

A spurt in open interest, accompanied by increasing prices, represents aggressive new buying and is bullish. On the other hand, expanding open interest in a downtrend represents aggressive fresh short selling and is bearish.

Falling open interest with rising prices represents short covering and is bearish. However, declining open interest when the prices are falling suggests that the market is beginning to unwind its short positions and can be taken as a bullish signal.

A breakout (either on the upside or downside) from a trading range will be much stronger if open interest rises during the consolidation. This is because many traders will be forced to cover their positions when the breakout finally happens. In short, the greater the rise in open interest during consolidation, the greater the potential for the subsequent move.

Closing Note on Indicators:

When you are a beginner, it's easy to start trading with indicators and candle stick patterns as they are very simple to understand and implement in live trades. However, most experienced traders are aware that indicators and candle stick patterns have a high probability of leading you into losing trades as they don't have a fixed stop loss point and the exit signal is always taken only after the candle bar period is complete (i.e., a lot of damage can happen in one weekly/monthly bar) which also means that we stand the chance of losing a lot. 'Only very few traders are successful trading indicators. However they develop their own custom levels and don't use the conventional levels which come standard in Technical analysis software. **Understanding indicators and candle patterns is important, however, resist the temptation to trade them, unless you have developed custom levels which have been tested for past performance in your chosen asset class. You have been exposed to better set-ups in this book; trade those.**

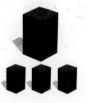

Exercises

Tools to supplement your trades

1)   *In a trending market we should use ____ as an indicator while in a trading market, where prices keep fluctuate between two price levels, we can use ____ as an indicator*

A) MACD, RSI

B) RSI, Bollinger Bands

C) RSI, MACD

Answer: ☐A

2)   *What should be the ideal indicator for Kraft Foods, an FMCG stock, trading in a band of USD 21 – 40 since 2003 (See chart below).*

A)   MACD

B)   RSI

C)   ADX

Answer: ☐B

RSI is the right indicator for stocks that are stuck in a narrow band for a long time. In the Kraft food chart, the RSI band is 39 – 63, which means we should try to accumulate till the RSI level touches 39 and sell when the level reaches 63.

INTEGRAL ASPECTS OF TRADING

CHAPTER 11

"Give me six hours to chop down a tree and I will spend the first four sharpening the axe." **Abraham Lincoln**

KEY FACTORS TO WATCH OUT

➜ Never trade futures and options based on spot charts, i.e. while trading options we have to look at options charts only and likewise for futures trades. Please note that options are subject to volatility in value (both time value and intrinsic value). The rate of movements of options prices will be faster when compared to futures or stock trades. Hence never trade options based on spot or futures charts. In fact, beginners are advised not to trade in options at all as the odds are always against you, even if you we get the price direction right.

→ If you are an office-goer, don't trade intra-day charts; restrict yourself to daily and weekly charts only as trading intra-day requires you to spend more time in front of trading screen than you may be able to devote. Further, the frequency of a new set-up emerging from charts within minutes or hours is higher in intra-day timeframes and hence, it requires us to adjust the existing trades or place new trades based on fresh set-ups. In the Nifty futures chart below, a bullish head and shoulders gives a buy signal. However, before hitting the target or the stop loss, there is another bearish head and shoulders, hence we square–up the existing buy trade and place fresh shorts in the direction of the new set-up we have on the charts.

Nifty intra-day chart

Fig 11.1

→ The opportunity on a daily or weekly timeframe chart is more significant than the opportunity on an intra-day timeframe chart, i.e. Irregular Diagonal on a daily chart is more important than Irregular diagonals on a 5 minute chart.

→ It takes a higher level of expertise to trade intra-day than to trade based on daily or weekly charts, as we have to take less time to spot opportunities in the intra-day timeframes than in daily or weekly timeframes.

→ The time taken to achieve the target level is less in intra-day timeframes while the point gain per trade is higher in larger timeframes.

→ Focus more on the set-ups detailed in chapters 3 to 7 of this book, as these patterns have a good performance track record across timeframes, asset classes and geographies.

→ Avoid trading an illiquid asset class. Low frequency movements in bid–ask rates and a high bid–ask spread reflect lack of liquidity. It's advisable to trade only in index futures or index stocks.

→ Never get confused with the setups or buy/sell signals that are generated by a different timeframe. In short, stick to the signals on the timeframe you trade in.

→ Set a stop loss level for every trade you enter. If the stop loss is taken out, you are out of the trade and you know that it's time to look for the next opportunity.

→ Never average down on a buy trade or average up on a sell trade.

A Step by Step approach towards success in trading

It's important to have a trading strategy before you start placing live trades. Hence it's critical that you follow a step by step approach. Firstly, go through the book till you understand the key set-ups in depth. After understanding the set-ups, identify them in price charts. As mentioned earlier, there are only 6 set-ups that contribute to price rises or price falls in any chart. Now try to identify them across charts (you will find one of the 6 set-ups mentioned behind every price rise or price fall in any timeframe, any asset class, any geography).

Half the job is done if you are good at identifying these patterns. Now, back test them on your favourite asset class and as you back test, you will learn to use these set-ups better. Then, in live markets, paper trade the best set-ups among those which have performed well in your back test. By now you will automatically have a trading plan and you will have conviction to implement your plans in live trades. The key challenge is to identify the set-ups real-time and to focus on the process alone; the proceeds will follow automatically!

Following a step-by-step approach towards trading success

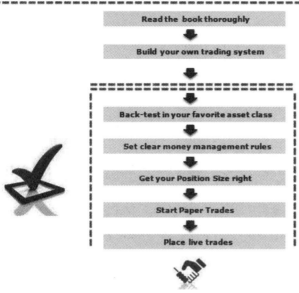

Now let's say you have a trading system which has been back tested for performance and you have undertaken paper-trading as well. Now you have the conviction to place trades in the live markets. Things can still go wrong, if you don't get your money management and position sizing right. Hence, apart from the performance of the set-up, it's also extremely important to plan the positions initiated per trade and have some basic money management skills before you start live trades.

MONEY MANAGEMENT

"Behind every successful person you will find a sound money management strategy"

Money management plays an important role in trading, as well as in daily life. Large institutions, like Lehman Brothers, Bears Stearns, etc., failed, not only due to their flawed investment philosophies but also due to improper money management strategies.

No matter how good your trading system is, it's inevitable that you will undertake losing trades and at times even 4 or 5 on the trot. The ability to take a loss and live to trade another day is the key to survival in the trading arena.

It's recommended that you do not invest more than 25 per cent of your savings in trades. You can expand your trading capital to up to 50 per cent of your savings only if you trade for a living and have/follow a trading system which has given consistent results over a sustained period as per your back test or in live markets.

For example, if you have USD 4,000 in your savings account, your trading capital should ideally not exceed USD 1000. Also in case your trading capital over time increases to USD 2000, adjust your position size accordingly. However, don't think of pulling in more capital from your savings account. If your trading capital goes below USD 100 from USD 1000, its time to revisit your strategy or stop trading completely.

Even within the total amount that you trade, it is important to plan out and identify the investments per trade. Usually, for futures and options (being leveraged instruments) it is not advisable to use more than 5 per cent of your trading capital per trade and for regular stocks, limit yourself to 25 per cent of your trading capital per trade.

Another critical rule: **do not invest or trade with borrowed money.** Leverage (borrowing money) is something you should avoid, as interest costs have the potential to erode your profits. In fact, leverage in trading has the potential to land you into a debt trap which is bad both for your trading success and financial health.

Ensure that you **get the best brokerage deal available** as slippages can eat into your profits or exaggerate your losses.

In a nutshell, remember that **money management and position sizing play an equally important role in trading success as developing and designing a good trading system.**

Position Size

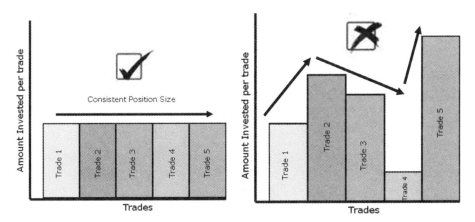

Fig 11.2

ALWAYS BE CONSISTENT:

Make sure that you place trades with consistent position sizes. For e.g., if you have USD 1000 as your exposure for each trade, ensure that you remain consistent with this position. Make amends to your position size only after careful evaluation. Then ensure that you remain consistent with the new position size. You can have five winning trades with a small position and you can lose all that money in the sixth trade, if you have a large exposure. That is why it is critical to maintain a consistent position size for the trades that you enter.

Time management is the fourth pillar for trading success apart from designing a trading system, position size and money management. It's important to manage your time during trading hours and post trading hours. For example, if you are an intra-day trader, zero down on the stocks you want to trade and try to restrict your tracking zone for potential opportunities to not more than 5 stocks. It's better to plan in advance and spend more time analyzing after market hours than during market hours as market movements can be so sharp that the opportunity is gone even before you spot it.

"Keep your emotions out"

It's important to note that despite limited entry barriers for trading, not many traders make the most of the markets. However, you can be assured of a successful trading career if you treat it like any other business and have a trading plan which constitutes the four pillars, while keeping your emotions out of trades. Also trade only when you find an entry as per your trading system, don't trade just because you have to trade everyday.

CLOSING NOTE

Statistics reveal that only 5 per cent of the trading community makes money in the market. Have you ever wondered why the remaining 95 per cent don't? The answer is simple: they don't follow a trading system. After losing money in the market, they tend to believe that trading is a risky business.

Risk, according to Warren Buffett, comes from "not knowing what we are doing". In fact driving a car for the first time is risky but as we keep driving it again and again, we reach a stage of unconscious competence. At this stage, even if we don't focus on driving, we know exactly where to accelerate and where to apply brakes because it comes naturally to us. This competence comes through practice.

The theory of driving is taught in driving schools and through practice we learn the art of driving. Likewise, though set ups have been explained with various case studies, this book is just theory and watching these set ups unfold again and again in live market just enhances our expertise.

Wishing you success in your endeavours!

More than 50 info-packed titles covering a broad spectrum of topics. Business empowerment and management insights. Entertainment and Music. Marketing and Finance. Stock Markets and Commodities and more.

FINANCE SERIES

☐ 1. What your Financial Agent will tell you and why you shouldn't listen	1 BOOK MRP : Rs. 299/-
☐ 2. Systematic Investment Planning - SIP	1 CD-ROM MRP : Rs. 299/-
☐ 3. Invest the Happionaire Way	1 BOOK IN ENGLISH MRP : Rs. 499/-
☐ 4. Invest the Happionaire Way	1 BOOK IN HINDI MRP : Rs. 299/-
☐ 5. Everything You Wanted To Know About Investing	1 CD-PACK MRP : Rs. 499/-
☐ 6. Everything You Wanted To Know About Investing	1 BOOK & CD ROM MRP : Rs. 599/-
☐ 7. Everything You Wanted To Know About Investing	1 BOOK MRP : Rs. 299/-
☐ 8. Mutual Funds Made Easy	1 CD-PACK MRP : Rs. 149/-
☐ 9. Market Guide (Hindi)	3 VCD-PACK MRP : Rs. 399/-
☐10. Happionaire's Cash the Crash	1 BOOK MRP : Rs. 499/-
☐11. ETF's and Indexing	1 BOOK MRP : Rs. 299/-
☐12. Financial Planning For Doctors	1 BOOK MRP : Rs. 499/-
☐13. Everything You Wanted To Know About Investing In Difficult Times	1 BOOK MRP : Rs. 499/-
☐14. A Trader's Guide To Indian Commodity Markets	1 BOOK MRP : Rs. 699/-
☐15. Systematic Investment Planning	1 BOOK MRP : Rs. 299/-
☐16. Happionaire's Money Game	1 BOOK MRP : Rs. 399/-
☐17. Everything you wanted to know about Stock Market Investing	1 BOOK MRP : Rs. 399/-
☐18. Retire Rich- Invest Rs 40 A Day	1 BOOK MRP : Rs. 399/-
☐19. Kaise Nivesh Kare Mandi ho ya Tezi (Hindi)	1BOOK MRP : Rs. 299/-
☐20. The Art and Science of teaching children about money	1 BOOK MRP : Rs. 499/-
☐21. Bill and Penny's Money adventure	1 BOOK MRP : Rs. 299/-
☐22. Retire Rich- Invest Rs 40 A Day (Hindi)	1 BOOK MRP : Rs. 399/-
☐23. Romancing The Balance Sheet	1 BOOK MRP : Rs. 699/-
☐24. 10/10- Now control Your Money Perfectly	1 BOOK MRP : Rs. 499/-
☐25. Investing In Commodities made easy (English)	1 BOOK MRP : Rs. 399/-
☐26. Investing In Commodities made easy (Hindi)	1 BOOK MRP : Rs. 399/-
☐27. Investing In Commodities made easy (Gujarati)	1 BOOK MRP : Rs. 399/-
☐28. Simplifying Financial Jargons with Professor Simply Simple	1 BOOK MRP : Rs. 299/-
☐29. Get Rich- A wealth Prescription for Doctors	1 BOOK MRP : Rs. 599/-
☐30. The Seven Steps To Get Your Dream Home	1 BOOK MRP : Rs. 499/-

☐31. Step by Step Guide to Investing | 1 BOOK MRP : Rs. 499/-
☐32. Everything You wanted to know About Stock market investing | 1 BOOK MRP : Rs. 499/-
☐33. Everything You wanted to know About Stock market investing (Hindi) | 1 BOOK MRP : Rs. 499/-
☐34. Everything You wanted to know About Stock market investing (Gujarati) | 1 BOOK MRP : Rs. 499/-
☐35. Plan Your Money | 1 BOOK MRP : Rs. 199/-
☐36. Plan Your Insurance | 1 BOOK MRP : Rs. 199/-
☐37. Manage Your Debts | 1 BOOK MRP : Rs. 199/-
☐38. Invest Your Money | 1 BOOK MRP : Rs. 199/-
☐39. Millionaire's Don't Eat Cakes, They Make Them | 1 BOOK MRP : Rs. 499/-
☐40. Happionaire Investment Secret for Women | 1 BOOK MRP : Rs. 499/-
☐41. Mutual Fund Guide | 2 DVD-PACK MRP : Rs.399/-
☐42. Jago Investor- Change your Relation with Money | 1 BOOK MRP : Rs. 499/-
☐43. Jago Investor- Change your Relation with Money | 1 BOOK & CD MRP : Rs. 699/-
☐44. Everything you want to know about Investing in Mutual funds | 1 BOOK MRP : Rs. 499/-
☐45. Fundamentals of Investing in Equities and Assets that | 1 BOOK MRP: Rs. 699/-
Create Wealth
☐46. Setting The Right Financial Goals | 1 BOOK MRP : Rs. 499/-
☐47. Romancing the Balance Sheet (Hindi) | 1 BOOK MRP: Rs. 399/-
☐48. Everything you wanted to know about Business & Economics | 1 BOOK MRP: Rs.499/-
☐49. Financial Instruments standards | 1 BOOK MRP : Rs. 1199/-
☐50. Make Your Money work harder by Monitoring Investments | 1 BOOK MRP: Rs.499/-
☐51. Spot the next Economic bubble | 1 BOOK MRP: Rs.699/-
☐52. Income tax for Doctors 2012-13 | 1 BOOK MRP: Rs.499/-
☐53. The only financial Planning Book you will ever need | 1 BOOK MRP: Rs.499/-

LEADERSHIP SERIES

☐54. Business Legends | 3 VCD-PACK MRP : Rs. 999/-
☐55. Dialogues With H H Sri Sri Ravi Shankar | 4 VCD-PACK MRP : Rs. 999/-
☐56. Business Legends 2 | 3 VCD-PACK MRP : Rs. 999/-
☐57. Dialogues with Deepak Chopra | 1 DVD PACK MRP : Rs. 999/-
☐58. Unlocking the Hidden Dimensions of your life with Deepak Chopra | 1 DVD PACK MRP : Rs. 999/-

LESSONS IN EXCELLENCE SERIES

☐59. Lessons In Excellence - The Indian Story | 9 VCD-PACK MRP : Rs. 1,400/-
☐60. Lessons In Excellence- The Future of Competition | 4 VCD-PACK MRP : Rs. 999/-
☐61. Lessons In Excellence - The Rule of Three | 4 VCD-PACK MRP : Rs. 999/-
☐62. How To Transform Business Through Gutsy Leadership | 2 VCD-PACK MRP : Rs. 799/-
☐63. Power of Impossible Thinking | 3 VCD-PACK MRP : Rs. 999/-
☐64. Lessons in Excellence - Cultivating an Innovative Culture | 3 DVD-PACK MRP : Rs. 999/-
☐65. Lessons in Excellence -Transforming companies through an innovative culture | 2 DVD-PACK MRP : Rs. 999/-
☐66. Lessons in Excellence- Competency Dependence: The Curse of Incumbency | 2 DVD-PACK MRP : Rs. 999/-
☐67. Lessons in Excellence-The Leader's Intuition | 1 DVD-PACK MRP : Rs. 999/-

ORIENTAL AND OCCIDENTAL SERIES

☐68. Global Investment Gurus Focus on India | 4 VCD-PACK MRP : Rs. 600/-
☐69. Investment Myths & Truths Unmasked by the wise men of finance | 4 VCD-PACK MRP : Rs. 600/-

CLASSROOM SERIES

☐70. Classroom - Series 1 - Answer To Where Do I Invest | 3 VCD-PACK MRP : Rs. 600/-
☐71. Classroom - Series 2 - Technical Analysis | 3 VCD-PACK MRP : Rs. 600/-
☐72. Classroom - Series 3 - Classroom with Masters | 3 VCD-PACK MRP : Rs. 600/-

CNN-IBN

☐73. 10 Defining Moments | 1 DVD-PACK MRP : Rs. 499/-
☐74. 60 Years Of Indian Sports | 2 DVD-PACK MRP : Rs. 599/-
☐75. Brands That Made India | 1 DVD-PACK MRP : Rs. 1499/-
☐76. 60 years of Cinema | 2 DVD PACK MRP : Rs. 599/-
☐77. 60 Yrs of Indian Music | 1 DVD PACK MRP : Rs. 499/-
☐78. Being- Business Leaders | 3 DVD PACK MRP : Rs. 499/-
☐79. Being- Directors Special | 3 DVD PACK MRP : Rs. 499/-

☐80. Being- Stars Special | 3 DVD PACK MRP : Rs. 499/
☐81. Being- Best of Being | 1 DVD PACK MRP : Rs. 299/-
☐82. Golden Generation of Indian Cricket | 2 DVD PACK MRP : Rs. 399/-
☐83. Heroes of India | 1 DVD PACK MRP :Rs. 299/-
☐84. 60 Hours - 26/11 | 1 DVD PACK MRP : Rs. 599/-
☐85. Secret Kitchens -India | 2 DVD PACK MRP : Rs. 399/-
☐86. Serret Kitchens -International | 2 DVD Pack MRP : Rs. 399/-
☐87. Makers Of India | 1 DVD PACK MRP : Rs. 299/-
☐88. Zindagi live | 6 DVD-PACK MRP : Rs.399/-
☐89. Bollywood Blockbuster Divas | 2 DVD MRP : Rs. 499/-

WIZARDS OF DALAL STREET SERIES

☐90. Wizards of Daial Street | 3 VCD-PACK MRP : Rs. 600/-
☐91. Wizards of Dalal Street Gen Next - Series 1 | 2 VCD-PACK MRP : Rs. 600/-
☐92. Wizards of Dalal Street Gen Next - Series 2 | 2 VCD-PACK MRP : Rs. 600/-
☐93. Wizards of Dalal Street Series 2 | 2 VCD-PACK MRP : Rs. 600/-

OTHERS

☐94. Time Management | 1 CD-PACK MRP : Rs. 199/-
☐95. Rules of M&A Game | 6 VCD-PACK MRP : Rs. 1400/-
☐96. The A list of B-Schools | 1 BOOK MRP : Rs. 249/-
☐97. Infrastructure - History of the future | 1 BOOK MRP : Rs. 999/-
☐98. Dream Decade | 2 DVD-PACK MRP : Rs. 999/-
☐99. Essentials of Communication skills | 1 cd Rom MRP: Rs. 299/-
☐100. Essentials Of Presentation skills | 1 cd Rom MRP: Rs. 299/-
☐101. Essentials Of Time Management | 1 cd Rom MRP: Rs. 299/-
☐102. Essentials Of Financial Accounting | 1 cd Rom MRP: Rs.299/-

NEW

☐103. Money Mantra Your Guide to Financial Success | 1 Book MRP: Rs. 225/-
☐104. 16 Personal Finance Principles Every Investor Must Know | 1 Book MRP: Rs. 499/-
☐105. Die Poor or Live Rich | 1 Book MRP: Rs. 499/-
☐106. Technical Analysis Trading, Making Money with Charts | 1 Book MRP: Rs. 599/-
☐107. Investing and Taxation for NRI's made easy | 1 Book MRP: Rs. 499/-
☐108. How to be Your Own Financial Planner in 10 Steps | 1 Book MRP: Rs. 499/-

HOW TO ORDER :

Call us: +91 99303 51413   OR   **E-mail us at:** cd@network18online.com   OR   **SMS:** 'CD' to 51818
Order by post...

Order Form

Name : _____

Address : _____

City : _____   Pin : _____

State : _____

Tel (O): ☐☐☐☐☐☐☐☐☐☐   Tel (R) : ☐☐☐☐☐☐☐☐☐☐☐

Mob: ☐☐ + ☐☐☐☐☐☐☐☐☐☐

E-mail : _____

DD/Cheque in favour of 'Network 18 Publications Ltd.' No. _____

Date : ____/____/_____   Total Amount Rs. : _____

Rs. In Words : _____

Signature : _____

Send it to :
The Manager (Mail Order) CNBC ,
Bestsellers 18, Network 18 Publications Ltd.,
Empire Complex, 1st Floor,
414 Senapati Bapat Marg,
Lower Parel, Mumbai - 400 013. India.
Tel.: 91-22-6666 7777